THE SHADOW OF EAGLE ROCK

When Cap Millet saves rancher Joe Grinley from being rolled in barbed-wire he becomes involved in a range feud. Later Joe's murder makes Cap determined to help Joe's family keep their ranch. The contest for water rights takes on an unexpected turn when Joe's son, Sam, is accused of murder and goes on the run. In a three-sided race to find Sam, Cap is opposed by the law and by those who want to silence Sam. The final showdown and Sam's emergence into manhood reach an exciting climax in the shadow of Eagle Rock.

THE SHADOW OF EAGLE ROCK

The Shadow of Eagle Rock

by

Jim Bowden

Dales Large Print Books
Long Preston, North Yorkshire,
BD23 4ND, England.

British Library Cataloguing in Publication Data.

Bowden, Jim
    The shadow of Eagle Rock.

    A catalogue record of this book is
    available from the British Library

    ISBN   978-1-84262-822-5 pbk

First published in Great Britain 1982 by Robert Hale Limited

Copyright © Jim Bowden 1982

Cover illustration © Michael Thomas

The moral right of the author has been asserted

Published in Large Print 2011 by arrangement with
Mr W. D. Spence

Dales Large Print is an imprint of Library Magna Books Ltd.

Printed and bound in Great Britain by
T.J. (International) Ltd., Cornwall, PL28 8RW

ONE

Cap Millet eased himself in the saddle as he halted his horse at the top of the rise. Both man and animal welcomed the touch of the gentle breeze on the higher ground after the heat of the valley. He removed his battered, stained Stetson, wiped the sweat from his forehead with his red, cotton bandana and then ran the cloth over his face, burned brown from the lined forehead to the firm, clean-shaven chin.

As he idly rubbed the dampness from the Stetson's sweat-band, his sharp, alert eyes arrowed through the distance to two men who seemed exceptionally active on such a hot day. They worked fast, sinking posts and stringing something tightly between them.

Cap's curiosity stiffened with tension and his eyes narrowed, seeking confirmation of his suspicion. He took out his spy-glass, souvenir of his service with the Union Army, raised it to his eye and drew the activity towards him.

Barbed – wire!

Cap's mouth set in a grim line. He had heard how this invention, by an Illinois farmer, was sweeping through the range-land. It was leading to trouble as cattlemen, used to the open range, saw land being fenced, not only by farmers but also by ranchers grabbing at the chance to protect themselves from newcomers or to seize land which they had regarded as theirs even though it was open to their neighbours. Now, here was barbed-wire in Texas.

Although he had never seen any, the stories he had heard gave him an abhorrence of the deadly barbs. He saw them as a threat to freedom and Cap treasured his freedom. Since the War between the States in which he had lost his home and his wife, Cap had roamed and he sympathised with men who cherished the open range.

As he lowered his spy-glass, his attention was drawn by the dust billowing behind a horse being ridden hard. The man was urging his horse faster in the direction of the two men erecting the fence. Cap slipped his Stetson back on to his head and watched.

Suddenly the two men stopped driving a post into the ground and, after a quick glance in the direction of the rider, they dropped their mallet and post and ran to their horses.

A new tension gripped Cap. He sensed trouble. They had been scared off by the approaching horseman. Had they no right there? He raised his spy-glass again and received another surprise when he saw that the two riders had pulled their bandanas over the lower half of their faces. They swung behind a rise in the ground and Cap lost sight of them until they reappeared, now at a walking pace, keeping to the cover of the rise until they were moving back towards the fence.

Cap swung his gaze on to the lone rider who was slowing his horse rapidly as he neared the section of the wire. Before the animal had halted he swung his lariat and laid a neat loop over one of the posts. He hauled the rope tight and at the same time turned his horse away from the post. His rope strained, and, under the urgings of its rider, the animal exerted more power until the wood gradually drew from the ground. The man lost no time in releasing his rope and giving the same treatment to the next post.

Cap glanced back at the two masked riders. They were still keeping their progress slow, steadily approaching the section being destroyed by the lone man. Reaching the end of their cover they waited until the fence-wrecker, intent on his task, was out of the saddle, unfastening his rope from the fourth post he had torn from the earth. Suddenly they burst into the open and were upon the man almost before he realized it. He twisted round, clawing for his gun as he tried to rise from his knees but his movement froze when he saw the cold muzzle of a Colt pointing down at him.

One rider slipped quickly from the saddle while the other held the gun steady, with never a waver to give the man a moment to seize the initiative. His gun was jerked unceremoniously from his holster and flung across the grassland. Before he realized what was happening gloved hands were wrapping barbed-wire around him. He started to struggle but the menacing gun stilled him. His assailant flung him to the ground and started to roll him into the treacherous barbs which bit into his flesh.

Cap did not wait a moment longer. As he slammed his spy-glass back into its leather he was sending his horse down the gentle slope towards the attack. Sensing the urgency of its rider's call the animal stretched itself to greater effort. The earth pounded beneath its tearing hoofs, jerking startled attention in Cap's direction.

The man in the saddle pulled his horse round and loosed off two shots at Cap. He was too far off for them to be anything but warning shots and when Cap ignored them the rider yelled to his companion who, startled by the disruptive action, had already ceased to bind the barbed-wire round the helpless victim. He raced for his horse and once in the saddle both men pushed their mounts into a fast gallop away from the scene of their attack.

Cap ignored them; the disabled man was more important. He was out of the saddle before the horse had stopped amid a swirl of dust.

'Keep still!' yelled Cap as the man struggled to twist out of the coils of cruel wire. In a moment he was on his knees saying more gently, 'Don't move. I'll get rid of it.'

Instinctively the man turned to look at Cap and the movement brought grimaces of pain to the man's face as the flesh-biting barbs tore at him.

'Hold it. Keep still.' Cap urged the importance of not moving. 'This ain't going to be pleasant for you.'

'Damn bastards!'

'Know who they were?' asked Cap as he surveyed the turns of the wire.

'No, but one had a rope burn on his neck.'

'Save it,' said Cap, when he saw that even talking upset the man's concentration to keep still. 'Tell me later.'

With two turns of wire round the chest and upper arms, a third around his stomach and another round his thighs, it was impossible to remove the wire without causing more pain but the man bit back the cries which wanted to be out and cursed the attackers to himself. The blood-letting barbs brought a paleness to the weather-beaten face of the man whom Cap studied between easing the pointed wire from the flesh.

He figured the man to be in his mid-forties and that the lines on his face had been etched by trouble. The eyes were dark, deeply socketed and Cap saw their keenness was slightly blunted, possibly by the drink which Cap could smell on the man's breath. There was courage in the man in the way he bore the pain and, Cap reckoned, in his unhesitating ride to tackle the two men. But Cap also read mis-judgement in that action in the way the man had not been suspicious of the ease with which he had driven the men away. He had been too intent on destroying the fence. Cap did not view his own ride in the same way. He was a stranger to the two men, they did not know his calibre, they did not want to risk identification by being caught. This man they must have known, knew his capabilities and wanted to teach him a lesson. They had succeeded until Cap's arrival curtailed them, but they had achieved something, maybe it would do. Better to get out while they were still unrecognized.

It took Cap almost an hour of gentle handling and tender persuasion to free the barbs with the minimum of pain. As the last one freed its hold on his flesh, the man let the tension run from his body with a deep expulsion of breath. He ran his tongue along his dried lips and looked gratefully at Cap.

'Thanks, fella,' he said appreciatively. 'Sure glad you came along.' He stuck out his hand. 'Joe Grinley.'

Cap took the hand in a firm grip. 'Cap Millet,' he returned and tensed himself against the pull as Joe hauled himself to his feet.

Joe winced at the soreness which pricked at his body. 'Figure I'd better get these looked at. Ride with me?'

'Sure,' replied Cap. 'I'll get your horse.'

Cap swung into the saddle and rode to Joe's mount which champed at the grass a quarter of a mile away.

A few moments later both men were riding east.

'Know who they were?' queried Cap.

'No.' Joe shook his head and pursed his lips with doubt. 'Been expectin' it, ever since that damned wire was invented.'

'First I've seen,' said Cap, easing himself in his saddle. 'Heard tell of it.'

'It'll come, bound to. Change the face of the land. And a damned bad day that'll be.' Joe spat with disgust.

'You run cattle?' asked Cap.

'Yeah. Circle T,' replied Joe. 'The line those two bastards were takin' with that wire would have cut me off from water.' His dark eyes flashed again with anger as the realization of what this would have meant bit into his mind.

'Who'd do that? Nesters?' queried Cap. 'Heard tell that, in some parts, nesters have really divided up the open range.'

'Right,' confirmed Joe, as they swung round a spur spreading from the line of the hill to their right. 'And there's nothing we ranchers can do about it, they're in their right.'

'Why not fence yourselves before the nesters move in?' suggested Cap.

'Best idea,' agreed Joe. 'My neighbours Matt Westwood, Running W, and Jim Dixon, Lazy Y, figure on doing it.'

'And you don't?' Cap raised his surprised query.

'Can't afford to,' replied Joe with a touch of annoyance and regret in his voice. 'Had a bad year last year.'

And probably drink too much, thought Cap as he recalled the whiskey-smelling breath of the man in the barbed-wire. 'Could those two hombres ride for Westwood or Dixon?' he voiced.

'Hell no,' retorted Joe, surprised by the implication. 'We're all on good terms, always have been. They're bigger than me but they don't hustle. Got together when we heard about the barbed-wire and what it could mean. They're going to fence but said they'd leave me open across to the water.'

'Likely to change their minds?' Cap probed.

Startled, Joe pulled his horse up sharply and turned his head to stare with a dark frown at Cap. 'You trying to stir trouble?' he rapped, his mind racing with the possibilities behind this question. 'You ain't in with

15

those two bastards are you? Planted so you could get in good with me to push a wedge between the ranchers around here. Nesters would love that situation.' Joe's hand had moved closer to his Colt. 'If you are I'll blast–'

'Ease up, Joe, ease up!' cut in Cap. 'I was just curious.'

Joe hesitated, a frown still colouring his stare. His eyes searched the stranger. He saw an open friendliness whereas he would have seen hostility at his tirade. Joe sensed that Cap was genuine in his concern. He relaxed, his hand drifting away from his Colt and back to the reins.

'Sorry,' he mumbled. 'It's just–'

'Forget it,' broke in Cap and stabbed his horse forward, putting an end to the subject.

Joe drew alongside Cap and they rode to the top of the next rise where Joe halted his horse again.

'That's it,' he said as Cap pulled his horse to a stop.

Grassland rolled away to the purple distance shimmering in the heat of the sun. A quarter of a mile away, sheltered by the gentle rise to their right, stood a long, one-storied, wooden house with a verandah

16

along the front. Beyond it was a smaller building which Cap judged to be the stables.

'Looks a nice place,' commented Cap.

'We think so,' said Joe.

Cap detected a note of self-satisfaction in Joe's voice. He glanced at him and saw that he had drawn himself a little straighter in the saddle and that the dullness in his eyes had been replaced by a gleam of pride.

'Figure you're surprised at it being all timber,' Joe went on. 'Hauled it all in myself, built it with my own hands. Determined to give Kate the house she'd set her mind on.'

'Good for you,' smiled Cap. 'Any family?'

'Two,' answered Joe as they set their horses towards the ranch. 'Sam, seventeen, and Abbe, fifteen. Lost two others.' With the last sentence a note of sadness touched his voice and Cap did not press for more information. 'Come on, meet 'em.'

TWO

The two men pushed their mounts into a quick trot and the sound of the beating hooves brought Joe's family on to the verandah, curious to see who rode with their man.

Cap saw the searching, questioning eyes slip from him and turn to Joe. Before they had pulled their horses to a halt in front of the house, Cap had made a quick assessment of the three persons who were there to greet them.

The light of curious interest in a stranger, who came with her husband, changed to one of pleasure at the return of her man, yet Cap felt he detected a touch of worried concern in her eyes. She was a fine figure of a woman, well made, her hips broad with child-bearing yet somehow she gave the impression of being gentle, for there was no domineering in the way she held herself erect. Cap read a fierce pride and belief in herself and he wondered if this had been honed on her husband's weakness for drink.

19

The girl had her mother's looks and Cap saw in the signs of the approach of woman-hood that someone would emerge who would have no end of suitors. Her smile was warm for her father and was not tempered by the shy curiosity for the stranger as her eyes constantly flicked towards him.

The boy stood tall and broad for his age, seventeen hadn't his father said? There was a defiant thrust to his chin and shoulders. His eyes were sharp, assessing and judging in a manner beyond his years and Cap wondered how much of that had been brought on by the fact that his father liked the drink.

Cap pulled himself up sharply. He was used to making quick estimations of people but he should not pre-judge the man he rode with.

'Hi, pa.' Sam welcomed his father as Joe stopped his mount beside the steps.

Joe nodded and tossed his reins to the boy who caught them deftly as he came down the steps.

'Joe! What's happened!' Kate's cry matched the concern and horror in her eyes as she stepped forward quickly to her hus-band who swung from the saddle. Her call came just as Joe's torn clothing and ripped

20

flesh made an impact on his son and daughter. Their anxiety equalled that of their mother as they pressed Joe for an explanation. The stranger was forgotten.

'Don't fuss, don't fuss,' Joe snapped but without any viciousness, for he was stirred by his family's concern for his welfare. 'Couple of fellas rolled me in some barbed wire.'

'Joe!'

'Pa!'

'I'm all right. Caught 'em erecting the damned stuff between us and the water.'

'I knew it would come.' There was a cry of anguish in Kate's voice, as if she foresaw trouble and could do nothing to prevent it.

'I stopped 'em,' went on Joe, 'but they doubled back and jumped me. Might have been worse but for Cap here.'

The mention of Cap's name startled the family, reminding them that in their anxiety they had neglected to welcome the stranger.

They turned to remedy that and found Cap standing beside his horse.

'I'm sorry, so sorry for ignoring you,' Kate, speaking for the whole family stepped towards him.

Cap lifted the Stetson from his head. 'Think nothing of it, m'am,' he returned with a warm smile. 'Understandable to show concern for your husband.'

'Kate, this is Cap Millet,' said Joe. 'Scared the two coyotes off.'

'Wish I'd been sooner,' said Cap.

'Thanks for what you did,' said Kate taking Cap's hand with a touch of warm, grateful thanks. 'You must stay and eat with us.'

'That'd be a pleasure m'am.'

Kate returned Cap's smile, then, in complete command of the situation, turned to her husband, 'Joe, I'd better see to those cuts. Abbe, see to the table. Sam, take the horses. Come along in Mr Millet.'

'Thanks. I'll help Sam first.'

'Leave mine, Sam,' said Joe as he started up the steps.

'Now, what for Joe?' demanded Kate.

'Gotta see Westwood and Dixon, tell 'em about this latest move with the barb.'

'It'll wait until tomorrow,' protested Kate. Cap saw the worry come to the pale blue eyes and a frown wrinkle the skin taut across her forehead.

'No,' replied Joe. 'The sooner they know the better.' He continued on his way into the house.

Kate hesitated a moment and Cap caught

22

the look of apprehension as he met her glance. Then she followed her husband quickly into the house. Abbe went after her.

Sam fastened the reins of his father's horse round the hitching rail and turned to take Cap's.

'I can take it Mr Millet,' he said.

As Cap automatically handed the reins to Sam he said, 'I'll come along.'

'Think I can't do it right!' Sam bristled. His eyes flashed angrily.

'Sure you can, son, sure you can.' Cap hastened his apology and cursed himself for acting so unthoughtfully towards the boy. 'Just figured I'd like to stretch my legs after being in the saddle.'

Sam made no reply and Cap knew the boy was still suspicious of his motive. Neither spoke as they covered the fifty yards to the stable and as Sam led the horse inside, Cap turned away to lean on the rail of the small corral in which three horses stood with tails flicking at persistent flies.

'I'm sorry, mister,' Sam muttered as he came to lean on the rail beside Cap a few minutes later.

'That's all right, son,' Cap smiled. 'Three fine horses you've got there.' Cap nodded at the animals in the corral.

'Yeah, Pa and I brought 'em in a couple of days ago,' said Sam.

'Help your pa with everything?'

'Sure do.' There was a touch of pride in Sam's voice, the pride of a youngster allowed to take on man's work.

'Good for you,' praised Cap, sensing the boy's resentment of Cap's earlier blunder evaporating.

Sam turned his head and looked curiously at Cap with questioning brown eyes. 'Cap? Short for Captain. Guess you were in the Army. Which side?'

'Union.'

Sam's lips set in a grim line at this information. His eyes narrowed, smouldering with a disturbing disappointment. 'Yankee!' The word was spat with a tone bordering on the edge of hate. It startled Cap to see it in one so young.

'Hold hard, son,' Cap's voice was steel-edged but it still held a friendliness. 'The war's long gone, five years, nearly six, no cause to still hold grudges.'

'Ain't there? You've seen my pa, must have smelt the whiskey.'

Cap nodded. 'Sure, but what's that got to do with the war, with the Union?'

'Pa fought for the South, was taken

prisoner and suffered bad in prison camp. Took to drinking when he got back to try and help him forget the horrors. Ma persuaded him to move West out of North Texas hoping it would help him forget. A new life in a new place. But it didn't. So money went on drink and we haven't expanded like we should have done. We stayed small while Dixon and Westwood grew.' A touch of fury had entered his voice and as he swung on Cap his eyes blazed, 'So ain't we got something to blame you damned Yankees for?'

Sam started past Cap but Cap grabbed him by the arm pulling him round to face him.

'See here, son, get things right,' snapped Cap, his eyes burning piercingly. 'Your pa may have had a bad time but he could have mastered the drinking if he'd wanted to. Others suffered worse, lost everything, even their families, but didn't take to drink. He was lucky he had you to come back to.'

Sam met Cap's gaze. His lips tightened. He snatched his arm away from Cap's grip, swung on his heel and hurried to the house.

Cap, wondering if his own story would have helped the lad, watched him go. Maybe not. The boy had a chip on his shoulder as

25

big as a tree. Besides why open old wounds for Sam's sake? Sam's view was no concern of his. He'd be gone in a couple of hours and that would be the end of the matter.

Cap walked slowly towards the house and had almost reached it when Abbe hurried on to the verandah.

'Mr Millet, food's nearly ready. Ma says if you want to wash draw some water from the well.'

'Thanks, Abbe,' said Cap with a warm smile which was returned with a touch of special friendliness.

Cap drew the water and slopped some into a large bowl on a rough shelf at the end of the house nearest the well. He quickly washed the dust and sweat from his face and hands. He slipped the bandana from around his neck and dried himself. Leaving the bandana spread out to dry, he returned to the house.

He found himself in a large room with three doors which he guessed led to the bedrooms. A table set for a meal stood in the centre and some chairs were grouped in a semi-circle around the fire-place set in the outside wall to the right of the door through which he had just entered. Under the window on the other outside wall there was a table with a bowl and other household utensils on it. The neat chintz curtains at the windows completed the woman's touch which made this room home.

'Come along, Mr Millet,' Kate greeted him with a smile as she straightened from the pan which hung above the fire. 'It's hot for a fire but it's how I have to cook.' She wiped the back of her hand across her forehead and flicked the unruly wisp of hair into place before wiping her hands on her apron.

'Cap, please. Everyone calls me that,' said Cap who noticed Sam frown at the suggestion. 'Did you get Joe fixed up?'

'Yes. He was not as bad as expected,' replied Kate. 'You'd done a good job disentangling him from the barbs.'

The door from one of the bedrooms opened and Joe, adjusting his shirt sleeve, came out. 'Sit down, sit down,' he urged indicating the chair at the table.

'You feeling all right?' asked Cap as Joe went to one end of the table. Cap pulled out a chair next to Sam on the opposite side of the table to Abbe.

'Yes,' replied Joe. 'Fit enough to teach those two cowpokes a lesson if I could lay my hands on them.'

'Who were they, pa?' queried Sam. 'Nesters?'

'You seen any around?'

'No,' replied Sam, 'but they could've moved in without me knowing.'

Kate was busy ladling stew on to the plates from the pan on the fire and Abbe brought them to the table.

'Didn't look like nesters to me,' Cap pointed out.

Joe gave a wry smile. 'They'll get up to all sorts of tricks to try to fox us. Had 'em before. Keep your eyes open son.'

'Right, pa.'

'And keep out of trouble,' warned Kate finally as she sat down. 'Don't go looking for it.'

Sam said nothing but forked some stew into his mouth.

'Mighty tasty, Mrs Grinley,' grinned Cap, appreciating his first mouthful. 'Ain't tasted stew like this for many a day.'

Kate smiled her thanks and asked. 'You got nowhere?'

'No, I'm drifting. Been drifting since the war.' Cap sensed Sam stiffen beside him.

'No home to go back to?' queried Joe.

'Had a small ranch before the war,' replied Cap, noting that Joe had not asked for whom he fought. Maybe Joe was like him wanting to get on with the business of living together and forget the grudges which had made brother fight brother. 'Had too many bad memories when I went back so I left it.'

Kate held back the questions which came naturally. She had no right to pry, just to satisfy her curiosity about the sadness which momentarily clouded Cap's eyes.

'What you been doing?' queried Sam, breaking a piece of bread to mop up some gravy.

'Job here, job there, mostly around cattle or horses. Took a drive up the trail to Abiline for a fella I once worked for after the war.'

'Get Mr Millet some more stew, Abbe,' said Kate seeing Cap spear his last piece of meat.

'Thanks,' said Cap with a grin. 'It sure is good.'

'Stay and try her flapjacks in the morning,' said Joe.

'Well, I–' started Cap with some doubt.

'Why not,' cut in Kate quickly. 'If you're just a drifter you may as well. Least we can do. Besides it'll do us good to have some company.'

Cap smiled broadly. 'Well, why not? Thanks a lot.'

With the meal finished Joe pushed himself from his chair, stretched himself, winced a little at the soreness of his cuts and said, 'Fancy a ride into town, Cap? I'm going to see Jim Dixon and Matt Westwood, they ought to be warned about that fencing attempt.'

Cap eyed the chairs round the flickering flames. 'Well, Joe, if you don't mind I'd like to savour the comforts of a home. You miss 'em when you're a drifter.'

'Sure,' boomed Joe, contented to let Cap have his way. 'You do that.'

'Must you go?' Cap read a touch of worry in Kate's voice.

'Well, honey, I figure Jim and Matt should know what happened today.' Joe crossed to the row of pegs beside the door and took down his Stetson, an act which put an end to Kate's attempt to get him to stay. She had been through this so many times before and she had given up making any great effort to stop him long ago.

'Hi, you two wash up for your ma,' called Joe as he reached for the latch on the door. Both Sam and Abbe already anticipating their father's usual words were starting to clear the table. 'Let her talk to Cap. Won't be late, honey.' Joe opened the door and strode out of the house.

Kate sighed, rose quickly from her chair and followed him.

When she opened the door again the sound of fading hoofbeats reached Cap as he took his plate to the table under the window.

'Like to sit outside a while, Cap?' she queried.

'Sure,' replied Cap and crossed the room to join her on the verandah.

Kate was standing by the rail watching her man ride away and showed no sign of recognising Cap's presence as he came beside her. He did not interrupt her thoughts. He recognized a moment in time which was hers and which wanted no intruders, but he wondered what lay beyond that wistful, thoughtful look.

The sun had lost some of its vicious heat and its rays were slanting lower across the grassland which rolled to the horizon, but still the awning above the verandah provided a welcome shade.

Suddenly, Kate started, her thoughts broken. She looked round quickly at Cap, but he was fractionally quicker and she never knew that he had observed the meditative gaze which followed Joe.

'Sorry,' Kate apologised as she turned from the rail and smoothed her hair back from her face. 'Sit down, please.' She indicated a wooden chair with a high back while she settled herself in a rocking chair.

'Joe sets great store by Dixon and West-wood,' observed Cap.

'Too much,' said Kate with a touch of regret.

'Friends from the past?' Cap asked.

'No. Only since we came here after the war. Joe looks up to them 'cos they're big, sees in them a dream he once held.'

'Once? What happened to it?'

'The war. Had a bad time. Was drinking when he came back and never gave it up. You can't achieve dreams that way.' There was sadness in her eyes as she looked at Cap and he was quick to note it.

'I'm sorry, I shouldn't pry. It's your private affair,' he hastened to apologize.

'I'm sure you weren't. It's all right. Maybe good for me to talk about it. Going to see Dixon and Westwood about that fencing was just an excuse. Oh, he'll see them, they'll talk about it but it'll be a drinking session. But they have the money.'

'And I'll have to go and fetch him home if he doesn't show up.' There was regret in the voice which came quietly but firmly from the doorway into the house. It was not a regret at having to help his father but a sorrow that it had to happen at all, when things might have been so different. 'Damned Yankees!' Sam spat those two words with venom as he turned back into the house.

Kate shot an alarmed glance at Cap and she realized something must have passed between the two of them at the stable.

'Sam!' She called with the tone of an offended mother's command. 'Sam, get out here!'

The door squeaked open slowly, matching Sam's reluctance to return, but he had a respect for his mother's authority and a love which regretted causing her any pain.

'Sam, your last two words could only have been meant for Mr Millet,' she said firmly. 'Now you apologize.'

'He's a Yankee. Fought for the Union. I asked him when I took his horse. And look what they did to pa.' There was protest in Sam's explanation.

'The war's long gone. It may have caused your pa to drink but he didn't have to keep it up when he came home. He just couldn't master it. We can't live with the past, son. It can't be allowed to distort our thinking.'

Sam looked at Cap. 'I'm sorry, Mr Millet,' he apologized quietly.

'Cap, Sam, Cap, everyone calls me that.' He nodded his acceptance of the apology.

'Hi, Sam, come and help me carry this coffee!' Abbe's call from the house broke Sam's embarrassment and he seized the chance to relieve the situation.

'I'm sorry, Cap,' said Kate as her son hurried into the house. 'He's a good lad, really. Don't know what I would have done without him.'

'I guess he is. I like him. Suppose it's natural when he sees the big ranchers and knows his pa might have been the same.'

Abbe and Sam appeared with mugs of steaming coffee and after giving one each to Kate and Cap they sat down on the verandah steps.

Cap felt himself drawn into the family atmosphere. His mind tumbled through what might have been and he cursed the blows which the war had dealt him.

'Ma,' Sam broke the peaceful silence. 'Those men that attacked pa, who do you figure they might be?'

'Don't know son. You seen any homesteaders?'

'No, ma. The last was eight weeks ago.'

'You could have missed them?' Cap's words were part suggestion part question.

'Sure,' agreed Sam. 'I can't be everywhere.'

'Pa can't have seen any,' put in Abbe. 'He'd have said.'

'And so would anyone else,' said Kate. 'Word soon gets around, Cap.' She added glancing at the man who stretched himself in the chair.

'Well, seems as though homesteaders are out. Must say they didn't look like homesteaders to me.' Cap caught the sharp glance exchanged between mother and son. 'You've some notion?' he added quickly.

'Well, nothing really, just uneasy feelings,' replied Kate.

'What ma means is we wouldn't be surprised if Jim Dixon tried to fence off the water.' Sam's words came out quickly as if he wanted to get something off his mind before his mother could stop him.

'Sam! You shouldn't accuse, we've no proof,' said Kate sharply.

'This is no time to hold suspicions back, not after what happened to Joe today,' said Cap.

'Really, Cap, we have nothing to go on,'

said Kate. 'It's just that we don't like Jim Dixon very much, never have, likes a lot of his own way. He's farthest from water and likely to suffer most if it was cut off. Westwood's near enough to the other fork of the river and is already running his wire to ensure his supply. Dixon won't want Westwood to outdo him. He knows we can't afford to fence so maybe...' Kate shrugged her shoulders. 'Well, who knows? But why are we burdening you with our worries. Sorry, Cap. More coffee?'

'Thanks,' said Cap. Abbe jumped to her feet and hurried into the house to get the coffee. 'Sometimes it does you good to talk of these things. What's Joe think?'

'Won't hear a word against Westwood or Dixon,' replied Kate.

'And Dixon out-smarted him on a couple of cattle deals,' rapped Sam, his eyes flashing with annoyance.

Cap glanced at Kate for confirmation. 'True,' she answered the look of enquiry. 'Those particular cattle would have helped us but Dixon wanted them even though he didn't really need them.'

'I figure he did it to spite pa after pa wouldn't sell out to him,' said Sam grimly.

'So, he's made a bid for your set up,'

observed Cap thoughtfully. 'And this could be another Dixon move.'

'It's a possibility,' agreed Kate, 'but I suppose there are others.'

Abbe returned with a jug of steaming coffee and refilled the mugs. The conversation drifted away from the possibility of trouble into talk of everyday things. The sun lowered, shafting rays of glowing colours across the grassland. A stillness settled on the countryside. The peace seemed too quiet.

Kate shivered. Cap's quick glance at her disturbed him for he saw anxiety brought about by premonition in her eyes. Furrows creased her brow and her face was masked, though only for a fleeting moment, by horror.

'You all right?' queried Cap.

Kate gathering her composure quickly mustered a smile. 'Yes. I suddenly felt cold. Must be the sun going down.'

'You want a shawl, ma?' asked Abbe.

'No thanks. I think we'll go inside.' She pushed herself from the chair. 'You stay if you want to,' she added quickly as Cap started to his feet.

'No, it's all right,' he said.

'Think I'll go and saddle my horse,' said

37

Sam, scrambling up from the steps. 'I reckon I'll have to go look for pa.'

'Like me to ride with you, Sam?' Cap asked.

'No. I can manage,' replied Sam. 'I've done it before.' His tone was cold, conveying the impression that he did not like the inference that he was less than a man and certainly did not like it coming from a Union man. He wanted no help from a man who had fought on the side which had made his father what he was.

'Sam, might be a good idea for Cap to ride along,' said Kate turning round in the doorway.

Sam shrugged his shoulders, an act of bowing to his mother's suggestion.

About to politely turn the idea down so as to respect the boy's wishes, Cap saw the anxiety in Kate's eyes as she cast him a pleading glance. He knew the worry, which had shown itself only a few moments ago, was still there.

'Sure, wouldn't mind a ride. Let's saddle up,' said Cap briskly and stepped from the verandah.

Sam's lips set in a grim line of annoyance as he reluctantly followed Cap.

THREE

They rode in silence. The sun lengthened the shadows of horses and riders across the dry grassland.

Cap held his horse back, just sufficient so that he could observe Sam but also to let the boy know that it was his affair. Sam was going for his father and Cap was not wet-nursing him.

Cap liked the way the youngster held himself in the saddle, alert, yet relaxed, in control yet letting the animal feel a freedom. Sam held to a pace good for both horse and rider. There was no undue exertion, there was no need, no hurry. Nothing was urgent about this ride and Cap realized Sam must have done it many times. The boy's face was set in a grim line. There was resentment in the expression and Cap knew that Sam did not want him along but that his mother's look could not be ignored.

Kate must have seen her son ride away on similar missions alone so why the concern this time? Why the pleading look, entreating

Cap to go along? Had the barbed-wire incident provoked a deeper anxiety causing Kate to fear some worse trouble? Cap wondered if there was any foundation for it. He didn't know enough about the ranchers' affairs to judge. Yet to subject a man to the torture of the wire spoke of an antagonism immersed in hatred or greed.

Cap's lips formed a question but he hesitated. Why was he getting involved? He barely knew these people. Owed them nothing. Yet he felt drawn to them. A loner drawn by gregarious instincts. A lonely man attracted by the family life which might have been his but for the rapacious murderers who had killed his wife after they had no further use for her. Or was it merely a desire to see justice done in face of the hated, encroaching wire?

He could turn away now, ride off and not be involved. He knew Sam would welcome that move, but Kate would be sorry, even disappointed that he had let her down. Cap kept his horse steady and voiced his question when they were half way to Pincher Creek.

'Anyone hate your pa?'

Sam did not answer. He moved not one muscle but stared straight ahead. Cap's lips tightened. It wasn't a chip on Sam's shoulder, it was a massive tree and it would take some felling. But it made Cap's determination to go along, to see this thing through, all the stronger. Maybe on the way he could make this boy realize the war was over and folk had to get on with living together.

'Sam, your ma wanted me along, you may as well deal me in, maybe there's something I can do to help.' Cap's voice was quiet but penetrating.

Sam still hesitated a moment and then glanced over his shoulder. 'There's nothing to do,' he replied curtly. 'Pa to find and take home. I've done it before. Don't know why ma thought I couldn't do it this time.'

'I don't believe she did,' said Cap crisply. 'She knew you could do it but I think she was frightened by the attack on your pa and was afraid something else might happen. That's why I asked if anyone hated your pa.'

Sam stared at Cap through the last remnants of daylight. 'You heard what we said back there. Jim Dixon could do.'

'If he did, could he hide it from your pa? Wouldn't it show? Yet your pa won't hear a word against Dixon or Westwood.'

'Booze, that you bloody Unionists got him

on to!' Sam's voice filled with anger and his eyes flared with hostility. 'That's why–'

'Leave that out of it,' Cap cut in harshly. 'The war's finished. Booze?'

'Yeah,' snapped Sam. 'Dixon and Westwood buy. They can afford it. Pa tries to stand his corner, but when he's spent up they still treat.'

Cap nodded. He drew the picture. A man looking up to the bigger ranchers because they had achieved something which he had dreamed about but hadn't attained because of his own, unrecognized, shortcomings. A man who had to feel big and did so by drinking with them and was blind to a contempt they may have for him.

'Wouldn't have been like that if the damned Unionists hadn't given him hell,' spat Sam.

'I said the war's over!' rapped Cap. 'Do you reckon Dixon or Westwood might use muscle to get access to water?'

'There's always been freedom to water.'

'Sure but the range is altering with the coming of the barbed.'

'Even so, Westwood will have water. But Dixon won't. He could be frightened that homesteaders will move in and cut him off.'

'Figure that's why he tried to buy your pa out?'

'Maybe, but it was a couple of years ago, before we saw barbed-wire.'

'Could have heard about it and anticipated what might happen,' said Cap. 'Did he outbid your pa for those cattle after your pa had turned down his offer for the ranch?'

Sam thought a moment. 'Yeah... Yeah, sure it was.'

'Maybe Dixon figured he'd make it hard for your pa and force him to sell.'

'Hi maybe you're right.' A note of excitement came into Sam's voice dispelling some of the resentment he had for Cap.

'Did he make your pa a second offer?'

'Don't know. He could have done without me knowing,' replied Sam. 'Pa wouldn't sell and now Dixon is using the coming of the wire to get us out.' A tension had come to Sam's tone as he voiced his suppositions. He grunted and lapsed into silence.

It was dark when they reached Pincher Creek which had settled down to its nightly ways. Lights shone from some houses, stores were closed and wrapped in darkness, and other buildings lay still in marked contrast to the noise which swept from the saloon.

There was no mistaking that business was brisk. Shouts and laughter rose and fell as

43

one cacophony of sound. It eased a little as a piano struck up loudly, to be followed by a great roar which suddenly stilled to leave a strong but plaintive voice sending its caressing tones to embrace everyone before drifting over the batwings to be caught by the timeless air. The few footsteps which clattered along the sidewalk seemed to tread more softly for fear of marring the song.

The two horses barely stirred the dust beneath their hooves as Cap and Sam rode slowly towards the saloon. There was no hurry. It was a song not to be interrupted. Sam's father would still be there when the song finished.

The night air was suddenly shattered. The notes from the singer were drowned, surfaced, faltered and then were cut short in the pandemonium which followed the roar of the gunshot from the alley at the side of the saloon.

Startled by the unexpected eruption of noise, the horses shied away from it, but their uneasy display was quickly controlled by their riders. A premonition seized Cap and the look in Kate's eyes flashed before him. He urged his horse forward sharply and was five yards ahead of Sam before the boy followed suit.

The batwings on the saloon burst open with a crash as people poured out on to the sidewalk. With yells and shouts they flowed along the boards towards the alley from which the shot had come. Curiosity brought heads poking from windows while some doors opened and more people joined those hurrying towards the scene of the shooting. It seemed as if the nature of the shots presaged tragedy and everyone sensed it.

Even as Cap hauled his horse to a halt and dropped from the saddle, the crowd were buffeting to a stop across the end of the alley allowing four men in front of the rush to investigate further. The air buzzed with questions and shouts as Cap elbowed his way through the crowd. He had to know. He had to be sure before Sam learned what he, Cap, felt sure lay in the alley.

He was almost at the front of the crowd when a yell came from the darkness. 'Joe Grinley! It's Joe Grinley!'

A coldness clutched at Cap's heart even though his premonition had prepared him for the news.

The name swept through the crowd like the wind through the prairie grass. As the name tumbled from lip to lip, Cap cursed himself for a fool. He had been driven on automatically by the urge to know, seeming to believe that somehow, by knowing, he would be able to break the news to Sam himself. Now the news would reach Sam and he was not beside him when he should be. Cap turned and pushed desperately against the bodies crowding towards the alley.

'Pa! It's my pa!' The desperation in the shout penetrated the noise which swirled with the crowd.

'Joe's son!'

'Sam!'

'He's here.'

'Let him through!'

New cries broke out one upon the other and, as bewildered minds grasped their significance, people parted to create a way for Sam. Cap found himself in front of the boy. He grasped Sam firmly by the upper arms halting his stride.

'Hold it, son,' Cap tried to make his voice firm but soothing, wanting to ease the truth into Sam's befuddled mind torn with a desperation to reach his father.

'It's pa! I've got to get to him!' The wild recklessness flared into anger at Cap's obstruction.

'Steady, son.' Cap tightened his grip.

'Get to hell out of the way!' snarled Sam. He jerked sideways and desperation lent strength to his movement. He broke Cap's grip and at the same time pushed him aside.

Cap staggered but regained his balance quickly to turn behind the youngster before the crowd could close in and separate them. Cap was right beside Sam when he reached the front of the crowd just as four men carried the still form from the alley.

'Pa!' Sam yelled as he stepped forward. The men paused. 'Pa!' Sam cried again as he stared down at his father. The eyes were closed, the head lolled to one side and the shirt was stained across the chest by oozing blood. Sam, wide-eyed, looked up at the men carrying the body. 'Is he…?' The words choked in his throat and, through the tears which were welling and dimming his eyes, he saw them nod. He heard with the dullness of a bemused mind their muttered, 'Sorry, son.'

A respectful silence had settled on the crowd which opened another way for the body to be carried to the saloon.

Sam followed in a daze. Cap kept close. The footfalls echoed unheard. The murmured speculations among the crowd were unheeded. The batwings squeaked mournfully as someone pushed them open and held them while the body was carried through into the saloon. The crowd shuffled in spreading itself around the room as the body was placed gently on a table.

Sam stood beside it, tears flowing as he looked at the face of the man with whom he had shared happy times. Cap held himself respectfully a stride away. It was best to let Sam have these moments.

They were suddenly ended when a door at the back of the saloon opened quickly and the town marshal, accompanied by a deputy, strode in. The deputy stayed by the door while the marshal moved into the room. Almost at the same moment the batwings squeaked and heads turned to see a second deputy step into the saloon and remain just inside the batwings.

Cap eyed the marshal as the lawman walked towards the table on which the body lay. He saw a well-made man of average height. He was not big but his body gave the impression of power, of a man in authority, a man who expected to be heeded. Cap judged him to be in his forties, though the lined, weather-beaten face could have added a few years to that estimate. He carried a Colt low on his right hip and Cap saw the long supple fingers were hovering near it. The marshal's deep brown eyes were alert, probing even though they seemed to be concentrated on Sam.

'Sorry, about this, Sam.' The marshal's words were quietly sincere. 'I've sent someone for the undertaker. He'll take care of things for you.'

Sam nodded. 'Thanks.' The whispered word almost choked in his throat. He stared at the marshal through tear-filled eyes. The respectful silence which had enveloped the saloon suddenly seemed charged with tension as the crowd saw Sam's body stiffen, his lips tighten, 'You gotta find him, Marshal!' The words came in a forceful rush, heightening into a crescendo. 'You gotta hang the bastard for what he did to pa!'

'We'll do our best, son,' the marshal replied.

'Best ain't good enough,' Sam shouted. 'You gotta get the damned bastard!'

'Steady, Sam,' Cap stepped close to the boy.

The marshal eyed Cap and seized on the opportunity to channel the talk away from Sam. 'Who're you?' he queried.

'Cap Millet. Rode into town with Sam. His folks have given me a bed for the night.'

'Yeah. An' if you'd come with pa when he asked you this mightn't have happened!' Sam swung round on Cap. His voice lashed at the older man and his eyes filled with an angry hate.

'Sam!' The marshal's tone snapped of authority. 'Cut it out. You ain't doing your pa any good with this.'

Before anything else could be said the bat-wings squeaked open and the deputy, positioned near them, stepped to one side to allow a thin man dressed in black trousers and black frock-coat to proceed into the saloon.

'Told you want an undertaker,' he squeaked when he approached the marshal. His hawk-like, long features seemed to register a delight that there was some business for him.

'Aye.' The marshal nodded over his shoulder at the body on the table.

'Right. I'll take him.' The undertaker motioned to two men to carry the body away. He glanced out of his eye corner at Sam. 'Tell your ma funeral day after tomorrow ten o'clock sharp.' He turned and scuttled after the two men carrying the body. He suddenly stopped, swung round on Sam. 'Sharp, mind you, sharp. Don't be late.' He scurried away leaving Sam, bemused by the suddenness of the parting, staring after him.

As the batwings swung shut after the body had been carried out the buzz of conversation, charged with speculation, broke out.

'Hold it! Hold it!' The marshal yelled. The noise subsided and everyone stared at the lawman. 'We saw nothing of the killer. Anyone tell me anything about what happened?' His gaze flicked quickly round the room seeking someone to answer his questions. 'You, Charlie?' His question was flung at the barman. 'Heard anyone threatening Joe?'

'No,' replied Charlie. 'It was the same as always. Joe met up with Jim Dixon and Matt Westwood. Sat over there at their usual table.'

Eyes turned to the table indicated by the barman.

'Where's Dixon and Westwood?' called the marshal, his eyes once again searching the room.

'They left,' replied Charlie.

'Before or after Joe?' asked the marshal.

'Before,' Charlie pursed his lips for a moment. ''Bout ten minutes.'

'Anything else?'

'No, Clint,' said Charlie.

The lawman nodded. 'Is that usual for Jim and Matt to leave before Joe?'

'Generally leave together, but I've known 'em go first leaving Joe to wait for Sam coming.'

'Any reason for 'em to go first tonight?' Clint asked. 'Quarrel, disagreement, anything like that? Anybody hear anything?'

A charged, expectant silence filled the saloon, as if everyone was waiting for someone to talk. Sam's fists tightened. He licked his dried lips. His eyes darted from person to person, willing someone to speak, willing someone to throw some light on his father's murderer.

'Aye. Aye. I did.' The timid, tentative squeak came from a short, tubby man who scrabbled his way forward through a knot of men.

'Oh my god!' The marshal rolled his eyes heavenwards. 'Spare me the town bum.' But he knew as lawman he would have to listen to anything which might give him a lead.

'All right, c'm here, Zak.' Clint glanced round the room. No one else was forthcoming. 'Everyone else get about your business. If you have anything to tell see one of my deputies.'

With the end of the marshal's announcement the saloon moved back into its usual nightly activity except for the small group gathered round a table indicated by Clint.

'No need for you to stay, Sam, unless you want to,' said Clint.

'I'll stay,' replied Sam.

The marshal glanced at Cap who nodded his agreement to remain with Sam.

'Sit down.' The marshal turned to Zak who stood nervously clutching at a stained, battered hat.

As Cap stared at the small man he wondered if he could really be trusted as a reliable witness or was he one of those who tried to be in the limelight but always failed miserably. His chubby, circular face was covered with two days' growth of beard. His round eyes were constantly roving with a nervous movement.

'Seat?' Clint pushed the question at the little man as he sank his own big frame into a chair. He removed his Stetson from his head and wiped his hand across his forehead.

'All right, Zak, what did you hear?'

Zak had seated himself and was perched on the chair as if his short, stubby legs could not reach the floor.

'I heard it. Mr Marshal, I heard it.' Zak's

voice came in short, sharp bursts.

'What, Zak?'

'I was sitting there, right over there.' He swivelled in his chair and pointed a small, fat hand with stubby fingers towards a table in a corner. 'On a chair with its back to the next table, the one where Jim Dixon, Matt Westwood and … and poor Joe sat.' He swung back to look at the marshal. His eyes widened as he said. 'I heard 'em, Marshal, I heard 'em.'

'Well, what did you hear?' urged Clint when Zak stopped.

'Ah, well, now Mr Marshal,' squeaked Zak, grinning slyly as he inclined his head towards the lawman, 'that would be telling.'

'Get on with it, man,' snapped Cap, wanting the information to relieve the anxiety which was torturing Sam.

'Hold it,' soothed Clint. 'It's the same old rigmarole with Zak.' He half turned in his chair and yelled, 'Hi, Charlie, bring a beer for Zak.'

'Coming right up,' called Charlie in acknowledgement of the order he had been expecting.

Cap stared at Clint. 'You mean Zak does this for beer?' he asked incredulously.

'Yeah,' replied Clint. 'He's done it before.'

'Then why the hell bother with him?' asked Cap. 'He may be spinning a yarn.'

'He might,' agreed Clint. 'But he might not. Gotta hear him out.' The lawman glanced at Charlie who placed a glass of foaming beer in front of Zak. 'Thanks, Charlie.'

A low chuckle came from Zak as he grinned at the froth and licked his lips in anticipation of the drink. Suddenly he looked up and his grin vanished as he stared at Cap. 'So you think Zak knows nothing. You're like all the rest.' He spat contemptuously. 'Maybe I'll keep it to myself and then you'll never know.'

'Hold it Zak,' snapped Clint. 'This fella meant no harm.'

Zak's round eyes swung on to the lawman. 'Who's he anyway? Why's he here?'

'Staying with the Grinleys,' put in Cap quickly. 'Name's Cap Millet. Rode in with Sam here. Forget what I said. Another drink on me if you'll talk.'

Zak put on a hurt look. 'Wal, I don't know.' He pouted. 'You said some hurtful things.'

'I'm sorry,' Cap hastened to apologize.

Zak hesitated. 'Aw, well, maybe I will.' He picked up his glass and drank. The glum look on his face changed when he tasted the beer and, with the thought of another glass, he beamed as he wiped his hand across his mouth. He leaned forward on the table as if to draw his listeners closer. 'Thirsty work talking,' he grinned.

Clint glanced at Cap with exasperation. Cap nodded and Clint turned towards the bar. Charlie, knowing Zak's ways, had kept his attention half on the lawman while he served his customers. He acknowledged Clint's signal and in a matter of moments was placing a second foaming glass in front of Zak who still leaned forward on the table. His eyes darted sharply round the others. He was enjoying the power he possessed and savoured it to the full for he knew that once he talked he would be a nobody again.

'Come on, come on, Zak, if you've got anything to tell us get on with it,' rapped the marshal irritably.

'Hold on now, Marshal, don't rush me,' replied Zak. He straightened and started to reach for the beer but Cap was quicker. His hand closed round the glass and dragged it away from Zak, slopping beer on the table. Zak looked up sharply. His eyes narrowed with a questioning annoyance.

'You talk!' hissed Cap, 'or else this beer goes on the floor.' He pulled the glass close to the edge of the table.

'Hold it, mister!' cried Zak. 'That's no way to…'

'Talk!' rasped Cap.

'All right, all right. The talk was nothing at first but then I heard …' Zak paused. His eyes fixed for a moment on the beer and then glanced sharply at Cap.

'Go on,' prodded Cap, inching the glass nearer the edge of the table.

Zak licked his lips. 'I heard Jim Dixon offer to buy the Circle T. Joe refused. Jim persisted in his attempts to get Joe to sell. Things got out of hand. Harsh words were exchanged. Threats were made.'

'Who by?' asked Sam sharply as his mind pounded with the implications behind Zak's words.

'Wal, son, I'm sorry to say Jim Dixon,' replied Zak, eyeing the beer again.

'What did he say?' queried Clint.

'Said there were other ways of solving things,' explained Zak. 'Your pa accused him of already saying that. Said two cowpokes had put barbs on him.'

'What did Dixon say?' urged Cap.

'Denied it, naturally,' replied Zak.

'What's this?' asked the marshal.

'I saw two men erecting barbed wire,' put

in Cap. 'They rode off when they saw Joe, doubled back and jumped him. They were rolling him in the barbed wire when I interrupted them.'

'Joe knew 'em?' asked Clint.

'No,' replied Cap. 'They'd covered their faces with their bandannas. But he did say he'd seen a rope burn round one of their necks.'

'Rope burn!' mused the marshal thoughtfully. 'Don't mean anything to me.'

Cap shoved the glass of beer across the table at Zak as he asked, 'Anything else?'

Zak's chubby hand closed round the glass eagerly. He drank long. 'More threats with Dixon storming off.'

'Dixon!' The viciousness behind the word as it hissed from Sam's lips startled both Cap and the marshal.

They glanced at the youngster and saw a hate and desire for vengeance cloud Sam's face.

'Damned Dixon! He'll pay for this!' Sam sprang to his feet and before Cap could stop him he was heading for the batwings.

Cap jumped from his chair. 'Quick one more answer,' he snapped at Zak, 'Was Westwood concerned in this?'

'Tried to calm things between the other

two,' replied Zak. 'Went after Dixon.'

'Thanks,' said Cap. He glanced at the law-man. 'I'll get after Sam.'

'Good thing,' said Clint. 'Don't want him doing anything stupid. I'll see Dixon, can't think he'd kill Joe.'

Cap hurried towards the batwings which were still swinging after Sam's departure. He sent them squeaking again as he pushed his way through to the sidewalk.

'Sam! Hold on!' Cap's voice ripped after the youngster who was making for his horse.

Sam took no notice. Cap thrust after him and grabbed him by the shoulder. 'Wait, Sam, you–'

Sam's eyes flared with anger as he shook himself free. 'Keep off me. That blasted Dixon is going to pay for killing pa!'

'You don't know he did it,' rapped Cap.

'Hell, you heard what was said in there.'

'That wasn't proof!'

'Good enough for me.' Sam started to turn but Cap stopped him again. Sam shook himself free. His lips tightened. 'I said, keep off me,' he hissed. 'Keep out of it. It ain't got anything to do with you.'

'It had since your ma wanted me to come to town with you,' snapped Cap, his eyes fierce with the intensity he felt about his

59

obligation. 'And I ain't letting you bring more trouble to her.' Even as he finished speaking Cap's fist sped like lightning to take Sam on the chin before the youngster had time to realize what was happening.

Sam staggered back under the blow and went sprawling into unconsciousness on the sidewalk.

Cap stepped forward and stared down at the boy. 'Sorry, kid,' he said quietly. 'It was for your own good.' He took a deep breath, bent down and dragged the silent form up and carried him to his horse.

Cap slung Sam face downwards over the saddle, unhitched the horses from the rail, climbed on to his own horse and took the two animals out of town.

FOUR

Sam's head throbbed and, with the slow return of consciousness, he felt as if a herd of steers was pounding over him.

The haze partially cleared, clouded again and then cleared a little. With it came a puzzle. His body was constantly jerking and he felt unnatural. He struggled to bring clarity to his mind to learn the truth. What had happened? Where was he?

If only the thundering in his head would stop. His arms hung limp and he was unable to raise his legs. Sam cursed his inability to get up. He fought against the almost over-powering force which threatened to take him into the realms of the unconscious once again. He beat it and sped the clearing of his mind. He forced his eyes open and for a few moments everything spun before they burst into a clear focus.

The ground. He was staring at the ground! Why was he jerking? It was like being on a horse and yet not like being on one. Puzzled he turned his head sideways. A horse! He was on a horse! He was slung face downwards over the saddle! Hell, what was going on? Then he was aware of the pain in his jaw and the events flooded back to him. His pa, dead. Jim Dixon to blame. Cap. Cap Millet stopping him, hitting him. And now this.

'Damn you!' Sam yelled. 'Haul up there!'

Cap stopped the horses. 'So you've come round,' he commented as he slipped from his saddle.

Sam felt relieved when the jerking motion stopped. He struggled to get up. 'Hi, come on, help me,' he snapped irritably.

'Don't get so hornery,' rapped Cap. 'Just calm down.' He stood in front of Sam who tried to raise his head to look at Cap.

'Hell, don't mess about, get me down,' snarled Sam.

'Boy, just ease your temper afore I do that,' replied Cap calmly.

'Damn you!'

Temper, temper,' drawled Cap irritatingly.

'Hell. Why didn't you let me get after Dixon?'

'To stop you doing something you'd have regretted and to stop you heaping more trouble on your ma,' replied Cap, emphasizing his words deliberately so that their full meaning would penetrate the young mind bewildered by what had happened. 'The law will take care of things, not you.'

Sam sighed with exasperation. He realized his position was hopeless. If he ranted and raved until dawn Cap would not let him off his horse and it was damned uncomfortable.

'You ready to calm yourself?' asked Cap when no comment was forthcoming from the youngster.

'Yeah, yeah,' muttered Sam with the reluctant truculence of youth.

'All right. See you do,' said Cap as he took hold of Sam. 'I don't want to have to hit you again.'

He steadied Sam as he helped him to the ground. Sam's head swam. He staggered momentarily and then, with strength and feeling returning to his legs, he straightened. He breathed deeply driving the muzziness from his mind. His jaw started to throb and he felt it gingerly.

'Sorry about that,' Cap said with a wry grin. 'There's always a first time.'

Sam grunted. He sized up the situation and for one moment thought about leaping for his horse and making a getaway. But he realized he would not succeed and no doubt

63

Cap would hog-tie him to get him home. He eyed Cap a moment longer then said, 'All right, let's ride.'

'Sensible thinking, son,' smiled Cap, giving Sam a friendly pat on the shoulder as he turned to his horse.

Kate Grinley hurried to the door. The sound of hooves was distant but she felt certain she heard them. Sam's back; Sam with his pa, she told herself. An end to the worried waiting.

With fourteen-year-old Abbe beside her, she stepped on to the veranda. The breeze whisked a strand of hair across her face. She brushed it back with long supple fingers as she stared into the darkness towards the now unmistakable sound of horses.

She inclined her head listening intently. Two! Cap Millet must have stayed in town. Even as she thought this she knew she was forcing it upon herself because it was what she wanted to be true. At the same time she laid a hand on Abbe's shoulder, a hand which was both a comforter and sought comfort. The touch and its implications startled her and yet it was a natural reaction to the premonition which had haunted her ever since Joe rode into town.

The horses came nearer, the soft sound of their hooves on the grassland ghostly in the darkness.

Kate's eyes strained for the first glimpse, the first recognition. Shapes. Forms. Sam! And … Cap!

Even though somehow deep down inside her this was what she had expected, it still came as a shock not to see Joe. Her body tensed seeming to steel itself for the blow which was coming.

'Ma, where's father?' Abbe's question came quietly to her.

Kate's hand closed a little tighter on Abbe's shoulder. 'I don't know,' she replied gently.

'Why hasn't he come home with Sam?' It was a natural query of a young girl who saw no reason for the usual to be changed.

'We'll soon know when Sam gets here,' answered Kate.

They fell into silence and watched the two riders approach.

Kate's eyes resting on her son, recognized dejection in the set of his body. She watched him intently as he and Cap stopped their mounts close to the veranda steps. Sam swung from the saddle and came to his mother and sister.

'Ma...' Sam's voice faltered. There was pain in his eyes as he looked at his mother, pain because of the hurt he was going to cause her. 'Ma ... pa's ... dead!' The silence stayed charged with that one word. 'Dead!' The word came again as a whispered confirmation. Sam saw his mother's face expressionless as if she hadn't taken it in and he thought he had a need to convince her. 'He was murdered!' His voice came loud, pounding the words at her. 'Shot by that bastard Jim Dixon!'

The mention of a name startled her. She jerked her unseeing eyes and attention on to her son. 'Sam! What are you saying?' Her eyes widened and her voice rose.

'Jim Dixon killed pa!'

'Pa's not dead, not dead!' The protest came shrilly from Abbe.

Kate drew her close as Sam glanced down at his sister and said, 'He is, Abbe, he is.' He looked back at his mother and repeated his assertion, 'Dixon killed him.'

'Hold on, son,' called Cap who had watched the scene in silence from the saddle. He swung to the ground and stepped up on to the veranda. 'You can't be certain about Dixon.' His voice was calm, steady, definite with fact.

'You were there, you heard what was said.' Sam's tone flared with anger. He swung back to his mother. 'Ma, he just won't have it.'

Kate looked at her son. 'You saw Dixon kill…' The voice, which had started calmly, faltered. The words caught in Kate's throat. She bit her lips to hold back the tears and steel herself against the cold, naked fact.

'No, Ma, I didn't,' replied Sam, 'but Zak Dillard told the marshal that he'd heard pa and Jim Dixon arguing.'

Kate stared at him. 'Then you can't be absolutely certain.'

'But, Ma…' Sam started to protest.

'I think we'd better all go inside and you can tell me everything,' suggested Kate.

Holding the weeping Abbe close to her she turned towards the door. She drew a deep breath as if summoning strength not to give way to her true feelings. As much as she wanted to shed tears for the man she loved she must not give way to her feelings in front of Sam and Abbe. She could have her cry in the loneliness of her bed.

Once inside the house, Kate turned Abbe to her and with all her love and compassion looked deeply at her daughter. 'Now, come, Abbe, dry your tears, pa wouldn't want you to cry.' She produced a handkerchief from the folds of her dress and gave it to Abbe. 'Mop them up and then go and make us a cup of coffee.' She glanced at Cap. 'Coffee all right for you?'

'Fine,' replied Cap.

'Then off you go, Abbe.' Kate glanced at Sam and Cap. 'Now sit down and tell me what hap...' She cut her words off when she saw Sam's face. 'What happened to you?' she cried in alarm, stepping to her son. She indicated the swelling and gash on Sam's face. 'Let me have a look.' She started examining the marks with a mother's concern.

'That was my fault, m'am,' said Cap quietly.

'You! You hit the boy?'

'Yes,' replied Cap, 'to stop him going after Dixon.'

'What!' Kate swung sharply on her son. 'You were going...' Her voice trailed away in the horror of what her son had intended to do.

'He killed pa,' cried Sam. 'The bastard deserves killing.'

'Mind your language, boy. Now, sit down and tell me all about it.' Kate was firmly in command of the situation as a mother who had to protect her son from his own cry for vengeance.

Kate listened without interruption to her son's story. She acknowledged Abbe's appearance with the coffee with a nod.

When Sam had finished she glanced at Cap with a look which asked if he had any more to add.

'Sam's told it right. I'm sorry I had to hit him. It was for his own good,' said Cap.

'I don't blame you for that,' said Kate quietly as she slowly stirred her second cup of coffee. 'In fact, I thank you.' She noted the momentary scowl on Sam's face. 'Some day you'll thank Cap for what he did. Your fool intention would only have caused more trouble.'

'But, Ma, Jim Dixon...'

'You don't know for certain, son,' Kate interrupted quietly but with a firmness that demanded her words to be listened to and heeded. 'You only have the word of a town drunk about what he heard. He may have heard what was said, but he may not. He could have made it up just to get drink.'

'We could ask Mr Westwood,' suggested Sam, giving voice enthusiastically to an idea which had just come to him.

'Yes, we could,' agreed his mother. 'But I

think the law will take care of all that.' She paused and looked hard at Sam. 'So don't go getting any more fool ideas about doing something yourself.'

'But, Ma, if we don't…'

'Enough, Sam,' Kate interrupted firmly.

'Ma…'

'Sam!' Kate's eyes flashed angrily at her son. She had every sympathy with his feelings but she dare not show it for his sake. Let him see that she shared some of his views and Sam would do fool things they would all regret.

Sam scowled, pushed himself roughly from his chair and stormed from the room. Abbe looked at her mother, saw the disapproving glare cast after Sam, burst into tears and ran from the room.

Kate sighed and turned wearily in her chair. She looked at Cap. 'I'm sorry about that,' she said.

'I know how Sam feels,' replied Cap. 'I'd have felt that way myself.'

Kate nodded. 'I guess it's only natural. I'd like to see things happening but it's up to the law. I can't let Sam run into things he can't handle.'

'Clint Holmes a good marshal?' asked Cap.

Kate pursed her lips thoughtfully for a moment then said, 'Yes, I suppose so. A little slow to act. Reckon Sam knows this and figures if things get delayed there's less chance of proving Dixon did it.'

'You think he did?' asked Cap.

Kate shrugged her shoulders. 'Could be. But I merely used his name. It could be someone else.'

'Anyone else likely to?'

'Not that I know of,' said Kate with a slight shake of her head. 'I suppose Joe has clashed with Jim on occasions but I wouldn't have said it would give rise to…' her voice faltered. She bit her lips hard to stem the tears as the turn of conversation brought back the realization that her husband would never be coming home again.

'I'm sorry,' Cap apologized sympathetically. 'I shouldn't be asking painful questions.'

'It's all right,' replied Kate, her voice low.

'Maybe you'd rather I rode on right away.'

'No, no.' Kate was quick to dismiss Cap's suggestion. 'It's good to have someone to talk to.' She hesitated for a fraction of a second then put a question tentatively as if she should not be asking it. 'You wouldn't stay a bit longer?' Then she added quickly so there would be no misunderstanding, 'I'm afraid of what Sam might do, maybe with you around he'd stay calm.' Cap studied his hands without speaking, and Kate pressed home her request with, 'You said yourself you were just drifting.'

Cap looked up slowly and saw the same pleading look which had silently requested him to ride with Sam into town.

'All right,' he agreed, 'but you must let it be on the footing that I'm helping out on the ranch.'

Kate brightened. 'Fine. There's quite a lot to do. Joe was going to start branding next week.' She got up and went to the door, opened it and called out, 'Sam, Abbe come in here.' She returned to her chair and a few moments later Sam and his sister came slowly into the room. 'I've something to tell you,' she said when they reached her. 'I've asked Mr Millet to stay on for a while and help out with the work.'

'I can handle it, Ma,' said Sam quietly without expression. He had to make his protest though he knew if his mother had made up her mind that was the end of the matter.

'I know you can, son, but it will be a lot easier with Mr Millet to help you, especially if we're still going to do the branding.'

Sam nodded without comment.

'Good. That's settled,' said Kate.

Sam turned and walked slowly from the room muttering, the words barely audible. 'Damned Union man.'

Admonishment sprang to Kate's lips but they remained unspoken when she saw Cap's signal to say nothing.

'Don't upset him any more tonight,' said Cap, as the door closed behind Sam and Abbe.

The following morning as they were having breakfast of beans and flapjacks and coffee Cap made a suggestion to Sam who had been silent since coming to the table.

'There are some corral fences need repairing, how about doing them today, Sam.'

'All right,' agreed the youngster morosely.

'It's a good idea, Sam, best to keep occupied,' said Kate. 'Abbe and I will take the buggy into town and see about the funeral. You said tomorrow.'

Sam went on spearing his flapjacks without comment.

'I figure if we do a good job on the fences we can bring in some wild horses. Saw some when I rode in yesterday,' said Cap. 'You could do with a few more horses and they can always be sold if you get more than you want.'

Sam looked up from his plate and Cap saw a small sparkle of enthusiasm in his eyes. 'You break horses before?' he asked.

'Sure,' replied Cap. 'Did a lot of it when I was in east Texas.'

Sam nodded and got on with his breakfast. As Cap drank his coffee he hoped he had made a step towards winning the boy's confidence and removing his antagonism.

The work of repairing the fences went well throughout the day. Cap saw that Sam was a good and capable worker. The youngster spoke little except about the matter in hand. Cap respected Sam's desire and kept in that way. He did not want to press himself upon Sam. Let the boy come round in his own time and of his own accord and by keeping him occupied the vengeance thoughts would hopefully fade away.

But Cap had reckoned without the funeral.

The morning was bright and clear with promise of a hot day as the buggy, carrying Kate, Sam and Abbe into town, stirred the dust. They rode in silence, each dressed sombrely to match the mournful occasion.

Cap, preferring to use his own horse, rode alongside.

The undertaker was ready, awaiting their arrival. A murmured word by him to Sam and the youngster brought the buggy round behind the flat cart which bore the coffin. The undertaker had covered the cart in black drapes and he himself had donned his black trousers, black frock-coat and top hat with black cloth tied round it to hang behind it to the collar of his coat.

He climbed on to the seat, picked up the reins and flicked them to send his horse forward. Sam did likewise, and, with Cap holding a little way back, the procession started along the main street. Word preceded it quickly and people were soon lining the sidewalks to pay their last respects to a man who, though not exceptionally friendly was known to them all and whose murder they abhorred. A few of them left the sidewalks to walk behind the buggy between it and Cap on his horse.

The vehicles moved with a mournful rattle, a sound which added to the grief which hung over the town as if it was trying to purge itself of a murder which shouldn't have happened. Men removed their hats as the cortège rumbled past. Women stared with sad curiosity at Kate who held herself erect and stared straight ahead, determined not to break down and give way to her feelings in public. Children were spoken to in a hurried whisper which stilled their fidgeting and left them staring in mild bewilderment at the sombre procession.

After the wheels had rattle past the main intersection of the street two riders moved slowly out and brought their horses alongside Cap.

Although Cap's glance in their direction appeared casual it took in their significant features. One man, broad, powerfully built sat heavily in the saddle. His square-shaped head, with short, bulging neck, seemed to be set into his shoulders. His size made his companion seem small, even though he was well-built, with a square-jawed rugged appearance. There was a toughness in his appearance and a self-assurance in the way he held himself in the saddle. His eyes were alert, missing nothing and Cap felt the coldness in them when they met his.

The make-shift hearse reached the lonely cemetery half a mile out of town. The undertaker climbed from his seat and greeted the four men, who had been waiting by the gate in the white paling fence. A brief word and they moved to take the coffin down from the cart.

Cap swung quickly from his horse and hurried to help Kate who was already getting out of the buggy. She nodded her thanks and Cap stepped away to allow her to join Sam and Abbe.

The procession made its way slowly to the grave and in a matter of ten minutes the burial was over. Those who had come to the cemetery moved away to allow the family their moment of privacy beside the grave.

Cap walked slowly towards the gate, a few yards behind the two men who had ridden alongside him. The broad, powerfully built man said something to his companion and then stopped, leaving the other man to continue on his way. Cap stepped past the big man and had walked a few more yards when he heard his name called. He turned to see Kate beckoning to him.

'Cap, I'd like you to meet Matt Westwood,' she said indicating the big man beside her. 'Matt, this is Cap Millet.'

'Pleased to know you,' Cap held out his hand.

'Likewise.' Matt took Cap's hand in a thick, broad, telling grip.

'Matt was concerned about how I was

going to manage,' said Kate. 'I told him you were staying for a while.'

'Sure,' Cap confirmed.

'Good. Bad business,' grunted Matt. 'If you need any help with anything let me know.'

Cap nodded.

'Thanks, Matt,' said Kate. 'I'll remember that.'

'Do,' said Matt. 'I'll be on my way. My sympathies again, Kate, to you and yours.' His glance included Sam and Abbe. 'Look after your ma.' He touched his hat and started to turn away.

'Mister Westwood.' Sam's words halted the big man.

'Yes, Sam?'

'You were with my pa the night he was killed. Did Mr Dixon threaten him like Zak Dillard says?'

Westwood eyed Sam for a moment. 'Zak say that?'

Kate, about to admonish Sam for bringing this matter up, held back her words when she caught Cap's almost imperceptible shake of his head.

'Mm,' mused Westwood. 'Then I guess there's no denying it. Dixon was annoyed because your pa wouldn't sell out to him.'

Sam's eyes smouldered with anger. 'There I told you!' he cried turning to his mother. 'I'll kill him! I'll kill the bastard!'

'Sam!' Kate's eyes flared with annoyance. She glanced apologetically at Westwood. 'I'm sorry about this.'

'Nothing to be sorry about m'am,' Westwood reassured her. He inclined his head slightly and moved away.

'So that's Westwood,' mused Cap when the man was out of earshot. 'The other Dixon?'

'Yes. He's heading for town now,' replied Kate indicating the man who was riding at walking pace.

By the time they reached the gate, Cap had noticed that Dixon had looked back several times, as if he was checking on something. Now he had halted his horse and held it in check as if waiting for someone.

Cap helped Kate into the buggy while Sam, after helping his sister, climbed on to the seat and took the reins.

'Mind if I don't ride with you?' asked Cap. 'I'd like to have a word with Westwood.'

'All right,' said Kate. 'Take me home, Sam.'

Sam flicked the reins and guided the horse across the grassland, away from town, to head for the Circle T.

As he climbed into the saddle Cap noted that Jim Dixon was still in the same position. Cap sent his horse into a steady trot after Westwood who had disappeared over the slight rise half a mile away.

Topping the rise Cap glanced back to see Dixon had not moved and a dust swirl rose behind the buggy heading for the Circle T.

Ahead of Cap, Matt Westwood rode at a steady pace. Cap tapped his horse into a gallop and soon the thunder of the hooves resounded across the grassland to attract Westwood.

He pulled his horse to a stop and turned it so he could see who rode in a hurry.

Cap eased his horse out of its gallop as he neared the rancher and slowed it to stop alongside Westwood.

'Howdy again,' greeted Westwood. 'You're in a mighty hurry.'

'Wanted to catch you,' replied Cap.

'Me?' Westwood's surprise also demanded a reason.

'If you want to be getting back, I'll ride along with you while we talk,' Cap suggested.

Matt grunted his agreement and turned his horse. Cap rode alongside him.

'Well?' demanded the rancher, eyeing Cap

from eyes which narrowed above the high, florid cheeks until they appeared to be peering from slits. He was not sure what to make of Cap. He was a stranger and yet seemed friendly enough with Kate Grinley. She had offered no explanation when she had introduced Cap and had left Matt wondering about him. The fella had an open, honest face, looked as if he led an outdoor life and must have served in the war to use the name of Cap.

'I wondered if you could tell me any more about what happened in the saloon, night of Joe's killing,' said Cap.

'No,' replied Westwood.

'Something you didn't want to mention in front of Kate and Sam,' suggested Cap.

Westwood eyed Cap suspiciously. 'Who the hell are you to be asking questions?' An edge had come to his voice.

'Cap Millet.'

'I already know that,' snapped Matt. 'What's your interest in Grinley?'

Cap hesitated only a moment. He saw no reason not to level with Westwood. 'I saved Joe from worse treatment from the barbs when two coyotes were rolling him in it. I was drifting. He and Kate offered me a bed for the night. I rode into town with Sam to

81

fetch Joe home after his session in the saloon. You know the rest.'

Matt grunted. 'And now you think you should look into the killing. That's the law's job, leave it to the marshal.'

'Sure. But there's no harm in taking an interest. Felt obliged to help Kate.'

'She sent you after me?'

'No. I figured it would do no harm to see if you could tell me anything else.'

Westwood eased his bulky frame in the saddle. 'All right,' he said. 'Jim Dixon tried to buy Joe out but Joe wasn't having any. Jim kept on and things got a bit heated. Words flew in anger but I reckon they were all said in the heat of the moment.'

'Dixon's tried to buy Joe out before hasn't he?' asked Cap.

'Sure.'

'What's he want more land for?'

'Doesn't really,' replied Matt. 'It's water he wants. Scared of homesteaders cutting him off if they move in.'

'Wasn't Joe scared? Why didn't he put up the wire?'

'Couldn't afford it.'

'Why didn't you all get together and fence?'

Matt smiled wryly. 'I'm situated near

water and I've fenced my supply. No need for me to run wire as far as the Circle T.'

'Why didn't Joe and Dixon get together then?'

'Jim figured he'd be paying for the lot and reckoned therefore Joe should sell out to him.'

'But Joe wasn't having any?'

'No. But Joe also figured that home-steaders weren't the menace we reckoned.'

Cap nodded thoughtfully. 'Thanks, Mister Westwood, I'm grateful. Sorry to have taken up your time.' He wheeled his horse and sent it across the grassland in the direction of the Circle T.

'Ma.'

'Yes, Abbe,' Kate glanced over her shoulder at her daughter on the seat behind her.

'A rider. I think it's Mr Dixon.'

Kate turned round on her seat beside Sam who, although surprised by the announcement, kept his attention on driving the buggy.

Kate squinted against the glare of the sun to look beyond the dust which billowed behind the wheels.

'It's Dixon,' confirmed Kate. 'Pull up, Sam.'

'We don't want to see him,' snapped Sam.

'We've got no choice, he'll catch us up,' replied Kate, ignoring the surliness which had come to her son's face.

Sam gentled the horse to a stop and a few moments later Jim Dixon steadied his mount alongside the buggy.

Sam's lips tightened. His stomach knotted and his heart started to race. He was face to face with the man who had killed his father. The man had the nerve of the devil to confront them now.

'Ma'm,' Dixon touched the rim of his Stetson.

Kate nodded. 'You riding after us?'

'Sorry to impose at such a sad time,' replied Dixon. 'I'm mighty sorry about what happened to Joe. He was...'

'Sorry?' Sam's word startled Dixon with its harsh interruption. 'And you did it. How can you be sorry?' Sam glared at Dixon.

Although surprised by the outburst, Dixon was quickly in command of his feelings. His dark, cold eyes, stabbed on to Sam. 'What you talking about, boy?' There was an iciness about his tone. 'Ma'm?' he added, looking to Kate for an explanation.

'Hush, Sam,' said Kate embarrassed by this sudden outburst.

'But, Ma, you know he killed pa!' cried Sam.

'Sam, we don't know any such thing.' Kate glanced at Dixon. 'I'm sorry about this.'

'Let the boy have his say. I'm mighty interested to hear this,' said Dixon. 'Well?' he demanded, turning his gaze on Sam.

'I know you had an argument with pa in the saloon. Zak Dillard overheard you.' Sam's words came fast. He felt he had to get them out quickly or maybe they wouldn't come.

'Zak Dillard! That old bum!' A derisive laugh added to the contemptuous expression. The amusement was replaced swiftly by a cold glare at Sam. 'You think an argument because your pa wouldn't sell the Circle T to me means I killed him?'

'You've tried to get him to sell before and there was trouble over the cattle you did us out of and the fencing a couple of days ago.'

'The cattle – I merely made a better offer for them.'

'To stop pa getting them.'

Dixon ignored the accusation. 'Sure, I've tried to buy the Circle T, I want to make certain of my water supply.'

'Yeah, that's why you sent two men to fence it off. But pa caught 'em.'

'I know nothing about it,' rapped Dixon. 'If your pa caught them then you know who they are.'

'Sam, your pa didn't exactly catch them,' said Kate wanting to ease the angry tension. 'Mister Dixon, the men rode off when Joe appeared. They came back rolled him in the wire but their faces were covered.'

Dixon glared at Sam. 'Don't go making accusations that ain't right. And for your information, the night your pa was killed I left the saloon before he did. From what I'm told, I'd be half way home before he left.'

'Anyone with you?' Sam spat the words at Dixon.

'No,' the man answered automatically.

'Then who knows you were half way home? You could have waited in town!'

Dixon's eyes narrowed. 'That's calling me a liar and I don't take kindly to it. If you were a man you'd be grovelling in the dust now.'

Kate took the threat behind Dixon's statement. If Sam opened his mouth again he'd be dealt with. She grasped Sam's arm tightly. 'Sam, hush up, now!' Her voice, though rapier-like in its thrust into Sam's mind, revealed her concern for him and expressed her desire that he should not heap more trouble on them.

Sam's lips tightened sullenly as he glared at Dixon.

'Thanks, ma'm,' acknowledged Dixon when Sam did not speak. 'Maybe now we can carry on our conversation.' Kate nodded. 'Ma'm, you're alone now, and I can't see you running the Circle T on your own. I'd like you to seriously consider selling out to me. I'm sorry to bring this matter up so soon but I wanted to be in before anyone else made you an offer.'

Kate hesitated a moment. She felt an extra tension come to Sam. She gripped his arm more tightly, warning him not to make another outburst at his resentment of being treated as of no consequence in running the ranch. She drew herself erect, meeting Dixon's gaze firmly. 'I thank you for your concern. There is no question of us selling. Sam and I will run the ranch.'

'But you can't do it on your own,' Dixon pointed out.

'I won't be on my own. I said Sam and I.' She emphasized Sam's name and she sensed the pride in her son at her confidence.

'And there's Mr Millet,' burst out Abbe.

Kate saw the puzzled query on Jim Dixon's face.

'The man who saved Joe from being barbed worse than he was. The man you rode beside at the funeral.'

Dixon nodded. 'Ma'm, he's a stranger, he may move on.'

'If he does, we'll manage,' replied Kate.

'It ain't going to be easy,' said Dixon. 'Remember I'll buy.'

Dixon vented his frustration on his horse as he jerked the reins hard to turn the animal and send it into a gallop.

Kate and her family watched him go for a few moments.

'Come on, let's be on our way,' said Kate, settling herself more comfortably on her seat.

Sam flicked the reins and sent the buggy into creaking motion.

'Ma,' he said quietly. 'Dixon threatened us.'

Kate lost in her thoughts about the incident, did not reply.

'Hi,' Cap greeted Abbe when she opened the door in answer to his knock.

Immediately he stepped inside the ranch-house, Cap sensed a tension in the atmosphere. He figured it was more than after-the-funeral stress when he saw the morose expression on Sam's face and the anxious frown which creased Kate's forehead.

'You had a visit from Jim Dixon?' queried Cap.

Kate nodded as she put down her cup. 'He caught up with us on the way home.'

'I thought he might when I saw him hanging back after the funeral.'

'Made an offer for the ranch,' said Kate, as she poured some coffee for Cap.

'He threatened us,' hissed Sam.

Cap looked quizzically at Kate. 'Did he?' he asked.

'Some would take it that way,' said Kate.

'I said he did. Ain't my word good enough for you, Yankee?' Sam snapped angrily, jumped from his chair and stormed from the room.

Worried concern clouded Kate's eyes. She looked apologetically at Cap. 'I'm sorry...'

'My fault,' broke in Cap, anxiously. 'I was clumsy. I shouldn't have sought confirmation of his opinion in front of him.'

'He's strung up,' went on Kate. 'He crossed Dixon. Called him a liar and a murderer. Dixon would have been rough on him but said he'd overlook it, Sam being just a boy. And that didn't please Sam either.'

'Want to talk about it?' asked Cap.

Kate nodded. 'I need someone to talk to especially with Sam in this mood. It frightens me!' Kate went on to relate the meeting with Dixon.

Cap listened without interruption until Kate had finished. 'So Dixon says he was on his way home when Joe was shot but has no witness to prove it. He could be telling the truth but he could be just as guilty, even if he wasn't in that alley with Joe.'

'You mean he got someone else to do the shooting?' said Kate.

'Yes,' said Cap. 'Westwood confirmed there was an argument between Joe and Dixon, but reckoned it wasn't bad enough to provoke murder.'

'But who can judge that?' said Kate.

'Exactly,' agreed Cap, and went on to tell Kate of his meeting with Westwood.

'What can we do?' sighed Kate staring at the dregs of coffee in her cup. 'It will be difficult to prove Dixon had anything to do with it.'

'It will,' said Cap. 'With you not willing to sell, Dixon could make another move. I figure we can only watch and wait and seize on anything that might give us a lead to Joe's killer.'

FIVE

Cap washed down the last of his flapjacks with his coffee and leaned back on his chair. 'That was good. Thanks,' he said with a smile at Kate. He turned his gaze on Sam who had been toying with his breakfast. 'Eat up, Sam. You'll need a full stomach if we're going to search out some mavericks today.'

Sam stared at his plate for a moment then looked up slowly to meet Cap's firm gaze. 'You figure we can get many?' he asked casually. As much as he didn't want to ride with this Union man, Sam recognized the fact that his mother was right in accepting help and that, as she had done so, it was maybe best to ride along, at least until he could do something about the whole situation.

'Sure we can,' replied Cap enthusiastically, seeing a chink in the barrier Sam had put up between them. 'Get a good start and maybe we can outdo Westwood and Dixon.'

'Right, let's go,' cried Sam, some eagerness returning to his attitude.

'Hi, finish off that breakfast,' called Kate, laughing at her son's impatience as he pushed his chair from the table and stood up.

Sam glanced at Cap who remained seated. The youngster quickly devoured the rest of his meal and said, 'Ready,' almost before he had swallowed the last mouthful.

As they saddled their horses, Cap glanced across at Sam. 'I'm sorry I upset you yesterday. I wasn't doubting your view.'

Sam shrugged his shoulders. 'I just wish folk would make up their minds. Sometimes they treat me as a kid, like you did asking ma, other times they expect me to behave like a man.'

'It's tricky at your age,' said Cap, 'folks forget.'

Sam jerked his shoulders again, as if putting an end to the matter, and bent down to tighten the cinch.

Cap let the subject drop. He figured that Sam, in his own way, had accepted the apology.

They spoke little throughout their ride to the east. About mid-morning Cap halted at the top of the rise and stared through the shimmering haze.

'Over there,' he called indicating cattle

scattered across the grassland to their left towards thickets beyond which the river bent in gentle meanderings. Cap studied the countryside with an experienced eye. To their right the rise climbed and sent a series of spurs stretching into the flatter land below. 'We'll make camp in that first draw,' said Cap. 'Bring the mavericks in there for branding.'

Sam nodded. He licked his dried lips a little nervously. He felt an excitement surge through him. He had ridden with his father but had little to do. Now he was being regarded as part of a team, a minor role, but nevertheless important. He could speed up the delivery of mavericks for Cap to ride down, throw and brand with himself doing whatever was needed in those stages.

They sent their mounts down the slope and once in the draw quickly set things the way Cap wanted.

Throughout the next three hours they rode, cut out mavericks, drove them to the draw where Cap roped, threw them and applied the Circle T brand. Sam admired the way Cap carried out the job with smooth efficiency, always in command, always the master, even with the most ornery of the mavericks. Sam worked hard and with a willing eagerness which Cap admired. He rode and handled a horse well. He cut out mavericks and drove them as if the skill was born in him. There were rough edges, he made mistakes, but Cap saw ability was there. He encouraged the youngster and though Sam said little he responded to that encouragement and Cap felt he had moved a step towards winning the boy's confidence and had taken his mind off his attitude towards Jim Dixon.

'We've done well, Sam,' said Cap as he removed the branding iron from the maverick's hide, stepped back and let the young steer leap to its feet and run. He dropped the branding-iron back into the fire, removed his Stetson and wiped his hand across his sweating forehead. 'Let's break and have some coffee.'

Sam welcomed the break from the branding and eagerly seized the coffee pot. He poured out two mugs and handed one to Cap.

'You ride well,' said Cap as he sat down.

'Pa soon had me on a horse,' replied Sam stretching on the grass. 'I've lived on 'em.'

'You catch on quick too,' said Cap. 'With help you could run a good ranch here.'

'That's what I figure on doing. Wish I was

a couple of years older.'

'You're doing all right.'

'You figure?' Sam eyed Cap as he sipped his coffee.

'Sure.'

'Yeah, but folks'll still think I'm a kid.'

'Behave like a man and they'll soon change their minds,' said Cap and added quickly. 'And I don't mean visiting the saloon and all that.'

Sam looked thoughtful but made no comment.

'Pity you can't afford to erect the barbed wire,' mused Cap. 'Maybe a bank loan.'

'Pa tried that,' replied Sam. 'Bank wouldn't. Thought him too much of a risk. Because of his drinking I guess.'

'Things may be different now,' said Cap.

'They wouldn't make a loan to me, they'd figure I was a kid.'

'Well, we'll have to see,' replied Cap thoughtfully.

'You figure barbed wire is the answer?' asked Sam.

'Not sure,' replied Cap. 'Could lead to a lot of trouble, but from what I hear it's coming to stay.'

Sam drained his mug and climbed to his feet. 'I'll get after some more critters. I'll head for the river.'

'Right,' said Cap. 'I'll see if there are any in these other draws.' He watched Sam hurry to his horse and admired the enthusiasm in the youngster. 'Careful of those thickets,' he called after Sam.

If Sam heard he made no acknowledgement. He swung into the saddle and sent his horse in the direction of the river.

Cap finished his coffee, tossed the dregs away and walked to his horse.

Sam rode quickly, eager to find more mavericks to add to Circle T cattle, his enthusiasm fired by talk of the future. Scanning the distance Sam saw some cattle disappearing into the thickets. He turned his horse in their direction and put it into a gallop. He eased the pace and rode alongside the thorny barrier which ran north and south.

The thicket of mesquite, scrub oak, prickly pear, cholla and tassjillo was impenetrable in some parts but thinned in others sufficiently to allow a passage, even though it was tortuous and unfriendly in the flesh-tearing thorns.

Sam cursed its hostile appearance but figured if he wanted more mavericks he would have to enter the thickets. He rode along the edge of the rough country, beyond which he knew, lay the river. If he was able to get in with the cattle, he'd be able to drive them back to the grassland.

Coming to a break in the barrier, a thinning of the mass of scrub and cactus, Sam stopped his horse. He viewed the situation carefully. It was hazardous but he figured he could make it. He scanned the thickets which seemed to challenge him with their defences of sharply pointed thorns. A movement! Excitement seized him as he narrowed his eyes to penetrate the dense growth. Cattle!

With no further hesitation Sam put his horse into the thickets. After the first few paces the animal became wary. Only under Sam's persistent urging and soothing encouragement would it continue to twist and wind its way deeper and deeper into the rough terrain. Sam became so intent on rounding the thicker patches of mesquite and scrub oak and avoiding the ripping cactus thorns that he lost sight of the cattle. He turned, swerved and veered so many times that he completely lost his sense of direction.

Pulling his horse to a halt he removed his Stetson and wiped the sweat from his forehead. He surveyed the situation. The thickets stretched all around him. He turned in his saddle. Which way had he come? Was it back there? Or in front of him? Over to the right? Where? A momentary panic gripped him. He was lost! He'd never get out of this cursed country! Then he crammed his Stetson firmly on his head and took a firm hold of his feelings. Don't panic. A man wouldn't panic, and he was a man, not a kid!

He settled himself back in the saddle and concentrated on extracting himself from the predicament into which he had ridden. He edged his way slowly, trying to keep tags on a general direction.

The sun beat down ferociously, seeming to concentrate on the thickets. Sam felt his energy being sapped. His shoulders drooped. His eyes stung. His limbs were sore with scratches from the sharp thorns. He could only be thankful that he was wearing chaps.

Sam jerked himself upright in the saddle. He cursed the sun, swore at the grasping thorns but drew back to himself a determination to find his way out of the thickets. He had to for his ma's sake, for Abbe, for the ranch, and to prove to Cap he was a man. He urged his horse on.

Half an hour later despair was beginning to settle a relentless hold on him when he halted his horse and raised his head listening intently. The excitement which had coursed through him for a brief moment was vanquished. Nothing. He had been mistaken. He hadn't heard voices. He licked a parched tongue across even drier lips.

Just as he was about to urge his horse forward his attention was riveted again. There were voices! He listened, his ears straining to catch the sound again. Yes! There! The distant talking continued. Too far to distinguish the words but nevertheless there.

Sam tapped his horse. As eager as he was to get out of the energy-destroying thickets, he kept his mount to a quiet pace. He dare not lose the sound of the human beings. Twisting and turning as he had to, he needed those voices to guide him in the right direction. His heart beat faster. He only hoped that whoever they were they would not move away.

Time seemed to drag. The voices seemed to get no nearer. Then suddenly the edge of the thicket was close. He stopped his horse and searched beyond the scrub. No one.

But he could still hear voices. Sam edged forward still guided by the sound. Then he realized that the open ground dropped away to the river, hiding the human beings who, unknowingly, had pointed a way out of the maze of growth which had threatened him.

He moved into the open with an immense sense of relief for he knew that he could ride to the south beyond the end of the thickets some two or three miles away and reach the grassland. But first he had to see who unwittingly had acted as his guide. With a gentle touch of his heels, Sam sent his horse towards the edge of the slope which ran to the river.

The elation Sam felt was swept into tension of horror when he saw Jim Dixon and four other men with barbed wire and fencing-posts. He jerked his horse to a stop and stared wide-eyed at the scene. His thoughts rushed madly at the implications. If the wire was run along the river and that intention seemed clear from the posts already erected then the Circle T would be cut off from water. Dixon knew about the fencing. It was his doing. Murdering his father hadn't paid off so Dixon was going to bring pressure to bear on them.

Anger welled inside Sam and overflowed.

Without any thought of what he was going to do he put his horse into a gallop down the slope.

The sudden sound of horse's hooves startled the five men who swung round sharply to see who approached. Hands closed round the butts of their Colts but remained there when they saw the rider was a boy.

'Stop that wiring! Get to hell out of here!' Sam yelled furiously as he pounded towards the group of men. He halted his horse amid a sliding swirl of dust in front of the men. The sight of his anger brought smiles to their faces except for Jim Dixon.

Annoyance clouded his eyes as he muttered, 'That damned kid again.'

Sam glared at Dixon. 'You're fencing us off from water!' he yelled. 'Get those…'

'We ain't,' interrupted Dixon with a snap to his voice.

'What the hell's this?' snarled Sam.

'We found it,' rapped Dixon.

'Found it?' mocked Sam with a derisive laugh.

'Yeah,' Dixon's voice had gone cold. He glanced at his men. 'That's right, ain't it?'

Agreement came quickly from every man.

'They'd back you,' snapped Sam irritably.

'You calling us liars?' Dixon's eyes narrowed.

'I know what I saw,' replied Sam.

'That's twice you've called me a liar!' spat Dixon. 'I warned you what would happen...' He let his actions finish his threat for, as he spoke, he stepped quickly forward, grabbed Sam, and before the youngster knew what was happening, tumbled him from the saddle into the dust.

Sam gasped as the breath was driven from his body.

'Grab him, boys.' Two men leaped forward at Dixon's command and yanked Sam to his feet. Dixon glared at him. 'I'm going to teach you a lesson you won't forget!' he hissed angrily. 'No one calls me a liar and gets away with it. I let you off yesterday because you were a kid. But twice! That's different. Figure you're acting like a man? Well, I'll treat you like one!' As he spoke Dixon was unbuckling his belt.

Sam struggled but he was firmly held. Sweat trickled down his forehead and ran down into his eyes. He blinked it away and as he tried to twist himself free glared at Dixon. 'You damned liar! You killed pa! I'll get you for that!'

'Tie him up!' snapped Dixon indicating

the nearest standing fence post.

'Barbed,' called one of the men dragging him forward.

His two companions grabbed a roll of wire and some clippers and followed the struggling Sam towards the post. The youngster pulled, resisted but could not overcome the forceful pull on his arm.

'Let me go! Let me go!' he yelled. 'I'll have the law on you!'

'Big man!' laughed one of the men as with a final tug they yanked Sam hard, face against the post.

He winced with the sudden pain and felt blood start to run from his nose. His arms were pulled upwards roughly and his hands slammed round the post. The men with the barbed wire and clippers grinned as they cut off a length of wire. Sweat poured from Sam's brow as he struggled against the steel-like hold. His eyes widened with horror as the barbs were raised to his wrists. Pain seared through as the men pressed the barbs into his flesh and twisted the wire round the pole. He screwed his eyes tight trying to shut out the torture. He bit his parched lips holding back the cries which sprang in his throat. He felt his legs grasped.

'Leave them. He'll not move far with that

wire round his wrists.' Though Dixon's orders brought little relief at least he would be spared the added torture of having wire round his legs. 'Shirt!'

Sam felt a hand grasp his shirt at the back of the collar. The sudden pull, which split his shirt, brought a cry to his lips as the tug was counteracted by the barbs in his wrists. Hands ripped the shirt from his back.

'Right, son. Now learn your lesson!' Dixon snapped the words at Sam. 'I ain't a liar and I ain't a murderer.'

Dixon's arm came back and forward in increasing momentum to send the leather slashing across Sam's back. The buckle curled into Sam's side. He jerked with the sudden pain, trying to move his body away from the agony but the pole held him. The barbs tore at his flesh under the movement. His head creaked backwards. His eyes closed tightly as he tried to force the pain from his mind. The leather swished again. The buckle drew blood. He bit hard on his lips to stop himself from crying out. Tears welled in his screwed-up eyes.

Again and again the improvised whip struck. Each time Dixon laid it a little harder. Blood oozed from the gashes, mingled with the sweat and ran down Sam's back to be diverted and soaked up by the remnants of his shirt hanging over his trousers. Each stroke brought fresh agony to his back and wrists until he could no longer hold back the tears. His brain pounded more and more with each convulsion. He felt his head going to burst. It began to spin. He dazed towards unconsciousness.

Hardly aware of what was happening he seemed to hear a rifle shot. A bullet! A bullet for him! That would bring relief. Automatically he braced himself as he had done against every other blow even though it did no good. He waited, tensed. The belt or the bullet? Nothing. What was happening? He forced some semblance of consciousness back into his befuddled mind. A voice! Not cursing him, not menacing him, but threatening.

'Drop it right there, Dixon!' The voice came from the distance, but it pierced Sam's daze. Overwhelming relief flooded his mind and as he slipped into unconsciousness his lips silently formed one word 'Cap.'

The rifle shot spurting dust, too close to Dixon's feet to go unheeded, froze his arm as he drew it back for another blow. Panting from the exertion of the whipping, Dixon

105

spun round. He glared hatefully towards the top of the rise.

Who the devil was stopping him from whipping this boy? Who was interfering in the lesson this youngster had to be taught?

Dixon's eyes stared malevolently from slits in his red sweating face and saw a man, feet astride, delicately balanced, with a rifle held ready for instant action. He stood at the top of the slope, silhouetted against the glaring blue sky like some avenger from another world.

'Drop it!' The order rasped again sharply, full of menace, leaving Dixon with no doubt about what would happen to him if he did not obey.

Dixon let the belt slip slowly from his fingers to lie snake-like in the dust. He straightened, clearing his mind of the punishment he had been inflicting to size up the situation and find a means of extracting himself from it. His eyes darted round his four companions and saw them frozen into immobility, not daring to move in case the rifle mistook their action.

'Unbuckle your belts!' The shout came above the almost unnoticed gurgle of the flowing river. 'Easy now!'

Slowly, each movement deliberate, so it

could not be mistaken, the five men un-
fastened the buckles and let their gun belts
fall to their feet.

'Kick them away!'

After only a moment's hesitation of surly
reluctance the five men kicked their gun
belts and holsters through the dust.

Cap, his eyes alert, his rifle held ready for
instant action, moved with a steady deliber-
ation down the slope.

'Over there,' rapped Cap motioning with
his gun.

The men shuffled together to the right of
Sam. Although it was now easier for Cap to
keep his eyes on them, he still kept alert.
One slip in his attention and he knew these
men would not hesitate to take advantage of
it.

'You and you.' Level with the group Cap
indicated the two he meant. 'Cut Sam
down.' The two men scurried quickly to do
Cap's bidding.

'Careful how you do it!' said Cap sharply
as one of the men picked up the wire
clippers.

With every caution one man cut the wire
the other took Sam's weight. They lowered
him gently to the ground laying him face
downwards.

'Remove the barbs from his wrists,' ordered Cap. 'Careful!'

As they eased the wire embedded in the flesh Sam stirred. The fog moved in his brain. A glaring light fought to replace it. His whole body felt weak, yet it seemed as if its full length was being supported. A sharp pain seered through him from his wrists. It came again, and again. Each time it sent more feeling into him, and drove away the bemused sensation in his mind.

His back hurt, felt raw. Where was he? What was happening? Mavericks, thickets, Dixon, barbed wire, belt. They all came in a series of flashes, penetrating his conscious world, bringing it sharper and sharper into focus. He was being beaten. He stiffened, waiting for the next blow. The ground. He was lying on the ground.

'Steady, Sam. Take it steady!' The soothing voice brought it all back to him. The last voice he had imagined when Dixon was flaying him. Cap. But this was real. Cap was here!

Sam forced his eyes open and closed them again quickly to shut out the glare from the fierce sun. Slowly he eased them open to see two men straightening beside him.

'Back over there!' Cap!

Sam saw the booted feet move from his vision. He turned his head but the movement sent hurt scorching through his back. Five men stood in a group but one impressed himself on Sam's vision more than any other. Jim Dixon! The sight sent anger coursing through him, anger which overcame the pain of twisting over and sitting up. He sat, his legs bent with knees up so that he could lean forward and rest his arms over them. His hands hung limp from the wrists. He stared for a moment at the ripped flesh from which the blood ran freely. Looking up slowly his eyes rested on Jim Dixon. They were filled with loathing as he hissed, 'Murderer! I'll get you for this and for pa!' He started to try to get to his feet but the pain seared through him and he sank back into his sitting position.

'Hold it, Sam. Sit still 'till I'm ready for you.' Cap's words came firmly. His eyes narrowed as he stared at the five men. 'Dixon you stay, the rest of you git.'

The four men scurried away quickly to their horses climbed into the saddles and sent the animals into a gallop.

Cap stepped towards Dixon who licked his lips nervously.

'You deserve the same as Sam,' rapped

Cap his eyes smouldering with a furious anger.

'No one calls me a liar and a murderer and gets way with it,' Dixon put on a show of courage even though Cap completely held the upper hand. 'He had warning yesterday.'

'What's this fencing?' snapped Cap.

'Like I told him,' replied Dixon nodding in Sam's direction. 'I don't know. Came across it just before he showed up.' He saw the doubt in Cap's eyes and quickly added, 'It's true. You've sent my men packing or they'd've told you.'

'They'd have backed you in any case,' retorted Cap.

A sharp intake of breath diverted Cap's attention to Sam. 'You all right?' he called, while still keeping an eye on Dixon.

'Just my back,' winced Sam.

His comment swung Cap's thoughts away from the fence and back to the immediate happenings. Sam had been hurt bad at the hands of this man who stood close to him. Suddenly, in a movement which sped like lightning, Cap brought the butt of his rifle round in a sweeping movement which caught Dixon on the side of the head. He staggered sideways, lost his balance and crashed into the dust.

Cap stepped forward and stood menacingly over the figure who sprawled in the dust. 'Like I said you ought to be whipped, but I gotta get Sam home.'

Fingering the side of his face where the skin had split Dixon glared hatefully at Cap. 'You, bastard, you damned bastard. I'll...'

'You'll do nothing,' interrupted Cap harshly. 'Now git.'

Dixon scrambled to his feet. Anger flared inside him but, under the threat of the rifle, he had to hold it in check. He grabbed his Stetson, straightened and glared at Cap. 'You'll pay for this.'

'Not if I get you first!' The words from Sam lashed at Dixon.

The rancher glowered at Sam, swung on his heel and hurried to his horse. Cap held his attention on him until he passed over the slope out of sight. Lowering his rifle he turned to Sam.

Black hatred smouldered in the youngster's eyes as he watched the dust disturbed by the horse's hooves, settling. A boy's mind, obsessed by his father's murder, had been scorched by a flogging. The deep anger had been turned into a malevolence. Now Sam's cry for revenge was not only for his father's death but also for the thrashing and humiliation which had torn away the last remnants of boyhood. Cap saw the eyes of a man turn on him as he stepped towards Sam.

Sam tightened his lips when he tried to move. 'My God it hurts, Cap,' he hissed.

'Sure. Take it easy. Let me help you,' replied Cap, extending his arm for Sam. Gently he helped Sam to his feet. 'Let me see.' Cap moved behind Sam.

The sight of the lacerated back made Cap wince. In many places the skin had been ripped and flayed into an ugly red pulp. Blood ran from the wounds, darkening the red weals across the rest of his back.

'Ain't much I can do here,' said Cap. 'Think you can ride home?'

Sam nodded. 'I'll make it,' he gasped with determination. 'As long as I can hold on.' He held up his hands for Cap to see the flesh torn by the barbs.

'Let's try,' replied Cap.

'Thanks for coming when you did,' said Sam, between the jabs of pain which came with each step towards the horses.

'Warned you about the thickets,' said Cap.

'Went after some steers, got lost.'

'I figured. When you didn't turn up I came looking.'

'Well, something came of it – caught Dixon red-handed with the wire.'

'You certain they were putting it up?' asked Cap, emphasizing caution by his tone.

'Hell, I saw 'em,' snapped Sam. ''Course he denied it.' His eyes flared at Cap.

'All right, all right,' replied Cap sharply and let the matter drop.

Sam sank his face against the saddle drawing deep on his determination to beat the pain. Sweat stood on his forehead with the effort of his walk.

'Like to try it?' asked Cap quietly.

Sam nodded and straightened. He grasped the saddle horn with both hands, sending knife-like jabs from his wrists along his arms. Getting one foot in the stirrup tortured his back. With help from Cap, he swung upwards and sank on to the saddle. Sweat poured from him with the effort, the salt-inflicting sweat stabbing sores as it mingled into the wounds. Sam slumped forward, driving strength back into himself. He must make this ride without any trouble.

'You all right?' Concern showed in Cap's tone.

Sam nodded.

Cap climbed into the saddle and turned his horse along the river bank. Sam tapped his animal and it started after Cap. Sam tried to relax, tried to fight the hurt but each step was filled with agony.

As they moved up the slope away from the river, Cap allowed his horse to drop back alongside Sam's. He was alert to the wounded man's needs, ready to lend a hand when needed.

Slowly, steadily, under the fierce heat of the sun which sapped at Sam's strength they rode beyond the southern end of the thickets, turned and headed across the long, seemingly endless grassland in the direction of the Circle T.

SIX

The big pan of stew simmered on the fire to Kate's satisfaction. She looked at the table which Abbe was setting. Everything was ready. No matter what time Sam and Cap returned, the meal to satisfy their hunger would be waiting.

She strolled on to the veranda, her mind flooding with the wish that she had been waiting for Joe and Sam. Sighing wearily, she sat down and gazed across the land fired by the late afternoon sun. The heat-baked earth sent air shimmering upwards sending a weird movement across the scene. How long she sat there she never knew but, when a different stirring across the dancing haze startled her, Abbe was sat at her feet.

Two riders! They were back. Kate straightened in her chair, her eyes riveted on the darker forms imposed on the landscape. Were they Sam and Cap? They rode slowly, ever so slowly. Strange. Someone else? But who?

Kate rose slowly from the chair and moved

to the veranda rail. Abbe came and stood beside her.

'Is it Sam, Ma?' asked Abbe.

'Don't know,' replied Kate, her eyes still fixed on the two riders. 'Too far away.'

'Why are they riding slowly?' questioned the girl.

'Don't know,' said Kate quietly then added, 'Hush now,' as if talking would wipe the figures from the quivering slate.

The riders moved nearer. Kate was suddenly aware of the empty feeling in her stomach. It churned, deepening, accentuating the numbness which gripped the rest of her body. Something was wrong. That dancing landscape mocked her, trying to hide something alien in the shimmering heat, holding back positive assessment until it was ready to reveal.

Then it hit her with a force which made her gasp. 'Oh, my God!' A figure was slumped in one of the saddles. The other was Cap. 'No! Oh, God, no!' Her face twisted with anguish, she swung round, down the steps and ran, with a pent-up fear of the worst clawing at her.

Her mother's eyes startled Abbe. In a moment of bewilderment she stared after her mother then she too ran. Two figures raced into the heaving landscape to finally merge with two riders in a motionless group which threw off the shimmering weave by their closeness.

'Sam!' Kate gasped and, in the moment's hesitation before she rushed forward to her son, she shot a wide-eyed look of horror at Cap.

Kate recoiled inwardly at the sight of Sam's back but drew sharply on her resilience to keep that feeling private. 'Cap! Abbe!' she cried.

Cap, reading a mother's anguished concern for her daughter's feelings, sprang from the saddle and grabbed the girl. 'Steady Abbe,' he urged, seeing bewildered panic in the girl's eyes. 'Sam's hurt, hurt bad. He ain't pretty.' Those few words were enough to ease Abbe's pressure on his hold from one of startled panic to one of desire to be beside her brother and mother. Cap let her go.

She stepped forward prepared to receive a shock but, because such young eyes had not seen anything like it before, the sight of Sam's back scared her. Her horror-filled eyes widened and turned to her mother. 'Ma!' Her long-drawn-out word sought comfort as well as posing a query as to what this was all about.

Kate held one arm out and drew Abbe to her. 'Sam will be all right,' she whispered. 'Now hurry home, get some water on the fire and turn down his bed.'

Abbe nodded, pushed herself from her mother and, with one swift glance at Sam, turned and ran for the house.

The voices came to Sam through a daze. The jolting hurt had stopped. He dragged his mind from the edge of oblivion. Forms swam before his eyes as he looked down. They swirled and were suddenly brought into sharp focus by his enquiring mind.

'Ma!' he gasped. 'Hello Ma.'

'Don't talk, son. We'll soon have you home.'

Home! The word sounded so good it raised a wan smile on Sam's face.

With his mother on one side and Cap on the other, Sam was escorted to the ranch-house.

Stopping in front of the veranda, Cap gently eased Sam from the saddle. With fussing concern Kate helped Cap take her son into the house.

Abbe had the bed ready and they laid Sam face downwards on the sheets.

'Ma, I...'

'Hush, don't talk now. Later,' said Kate, gently brushing away the hair which had fallen across his face. 'We'll get you seen to first.' Kate straightened and looked down at the sickening red which was her son's back. She forced the nausea away, examined his wrists and said quietly to Cap. 'I can only tidy him up and clean the wounds. He needs the doctor.'

'I'll fetch him,' replied Cap and turned for the door.

Kate hurried after him. 'Abbe,' she called. 'A bowl of hot water, a jug of cold and those strips of sheeting.' She halted Cap when he reached the outside door. 'What happened? Who did this to him?'

Cap quickly related the incident as he knew it.

'Dixon!' The word came with a cold menace from Kate. 'No one does this to my son and gets away with it.'

The threat came with such icy, calculated resolve that Cap was startled. He grabbed Kate firmly by the shoulders bringing her attention back to him. He stared into her eyes. 'Forget that, Kate, you look after Sam. I'll get the doctor and I'll see the marshal.'

'Ma, everything's ready.' Abbe's voice, added to Cap's, jolted Kate back to Sam's

119

immediate needs. She swung away from Cap and hurried to the bedroom.

Once Cap was in the saddle, he lost no time in urging his horse for Pincher Creek. He was thankful to find the doctor at home. Once in possession of the facts about Sam, the doctor lost no time in leaving for the Circle T.

Darkness was enclosing the main street when Cap hurried towards the light which flared and settled to burn steadily in the marshal's office.

When the lawman looked up from his desk to see who entered, he nodded his recognition.

'Marshal, I just took Sam Grinley home after Dixon had had him tied with barbed wire and had flogged him with his belt.'

'So?' queried the marshal.

Startled by the casual attitude, Cap snapped, 'Do something about it!'

'What?' returned the marshal. 'If I arrested every man for that sort of fracas I'd not have a jail big enough.'

'This ain't that sort of fracas,' roared Cap. 'Dixon whipped a boy!'

'Sam's word against Jim's.'

'I saw him, I stopped him!' thundered Cap. 'What more do you want?'

'Still your word against his,' replied the marshal, leaning back in his chair. 'And he'd deny if it if I tried to arrest him.'

Cap looked away in exasperated disgust. 'So if a man denies a charge you don't arrest him?'

'Depends,' retorted the marshal.

'Like whether you're in his pocket or not,' snapped Cap.

The lawman stiffened. 'You insinuating?'

'If it fits.'

Holmes hesitated a moment then eyed Cap. 'Being town marshal's my living. No man runs me. But I don't go around bucking the men who put me in. Besides, from what I heard, Sam accused Dixon to his face after the funeral, maybe Sam deserved what he got, that is if Dixon did it.'

Cap realized that no matter how he pursued the subject he would get nowhere. 'Well, tell me this, did you question Dixon about Joe's killing?'

'Sure,' replied Holmes. 'That's part of my job. If murder's committed I investigate.'

'Well?' Cap prompted.

'Doesn't deny there was an argument but doesn't admit a murder, says he was riding home when Joe was killed.'

'As expected,' commented Cap. He turned

121

from the desk.

'Millet!' The lawman's authority halted Cap as his hand closed on the knob of the outside door. Cap turned. 'If you got ideas to do some investigating – don't. Remember I'm the law around here.'

Cap met the marshal's gaze firmly for a moment then swung out of the office.

On his ride back to the Circle T, Cap had time to turn the events over in his mind but he got no nearer solving the mystery of Joe's death.

The doctor was still with Sam when Cap arrived at the ranch. After stabling his horse, he waited on the veranda until Kate and the doctor appeared.

'How is he?' Cap asked with concern.

'He'll be all right,' replied the doctor. 'That back will be sore for a long while but he'll be up and about in a couple of days.' He turned to Kate. 'See that he takes things steady. I'll look in tomorrow.'

'Thanks,' replied Kate. 'I'm grateful to you.'

The doctor crammed his black, low-crowned sombrero on his head and started down the steps. He stopped, turned and eyed Cap. 'I'm a doctor, I keep to that and try not to get drawn into any of these affairs, but tell me, who did that to Sam?'

'Jim Dixon,' replied Cap.

The doctor grunted. 'I ain't going to ask why, but have you reported it to the marshal?'

'After I saw you,' said Cap.

'And what did he say?' queried the doctor.

'Figures Dixon will deny it if he asks him, so why bother. It'll be Sam's word and mine against Dixon's.'

'But isn't he going to investigate?' cried Kate.

'Reckons he won't get anywhere, so why buck the man who put him in office.'

'It figures,' grunted the doctor derisively. ''Typical Clint Holmes. Straight enough but won't head for trouble. Has to be certain before he'll act.' He gave another grunt of disapproval and went to his buggy.

As the doctor drove away, Kate turned to Cap. 'If the law ain't going to do anything there's only one way to get justice.' The chill in her voice and the dark threat in her eyes alarmed Cap.

'Hold on, Kate,' he said, an edge to his voice. 'Don't go getting ideas about taking the law into your hands.'

'I can use a gun!' Kate snapped.

Cap grabbed her by the shoulders and

held her firmly when she would have turned away. He stared hard into her eyes. 'You'll only bring more trouble. Maybe get yourself killed. Then what would Abbe and Sam do?' His words were sharp to penetrate a mind which, at this moment, could only think of revenge.

'But...'

'No buts,' cut in Cap. 'You get this fool notion out of your head, you hear me?' Kate stared at him with unseeing eyes. Cap shook her. 'You hear me?' he repeated sharply.

Kate started. Her eyes focused on him. Tears welled in them, then suddenly overflowed. Kate sank against him, sobs racking her body.

Cap held her and let the tears take away the tension which had built up since Sam's arrival.

The sobs eased slowly and, when they finally stopped, Kate pushed herself away from Cap. 'I'm sorry,' she said, embarrassed, as she took a handkerchief from the sleeve of her dress.

'That's all right,' replied Cap quietly. 'It's what you needed. You'd held your feelings back too long.'

Kate wiped her eyes. 'Come, you must be hungry.' She managed a wan smile when she added, 'The stew will be well done.'

She turned for the door but Cap stopped her. 'No more fool ideas, Kate. Leave the nosing around for me to do.'

Kate nodded, her grateful thanks showing in her eyes.

'What today?' asked Sam when, two days later Cap looked into the bedroom before leaving the ranch.

'Might ride into the hills, see if I can locate any mustangs we can take when you are up and about again.'

'I'll be up when you get back,' replied Sam enthusiastically.

'Take it steady,' warned Cap.

'Doc said a couple of days, and I feel much better. Back's still sore, but it's mending. I'll put up with that to be on my feet again.'

'Good for you,' grinned Cap. 'See you.'

Once he had left the house, Cap soon had his horse saddled and was riding in a southerly direction. After a quarter of an hour he swung away from the distant hills and headed for the river. He figured that plenty of time had passed since the trouble for Dixon to start fencing again if indeed it was Dixon.

Cap kept to a steady pace, conserving his

own and his horse's energy. He mused on the chances which had landed him in somebody's else's troubles. Now, he couldn't ignore them and ride away. And what then, when the time came for him to move on? Back to his drifting? Back to being a loner? But those problems were in the future. Now it was a question of murder, fencing and flogging.

Cap came at a tangent to the thickets, skirted their southern edge and stopped his horse short of the top of the slope to the river. He slipped from the saddle, secured his horse to a low bush and crossed the few remaining yards on foot.

Below him the river ran away to his left. The barbed fence was still in position. As he surveyed it quickly he tensed and dropped flat. Four men were mounting their horses. They turned them and rode quickly along the river bank away from him. Cap cursed. Too far away to make an identification and too late to get near them.

Cap leapt to his feet and raced for his horse. He slipped the reins from the bush and sprang into the saddle turning the horse as he did so. He put the horse down the slope moving across it diagonally. He was half-way down when the crash of a rifle split the air. The bullet seared across the horse's neck. Scared, the animal tried to turn, lost its footing and crashed to the ground and tumbled over to slide down the slope, scattering earth and stones with it.

When the horse fell, Cap flung himself clear before it hit the ground. He fell heavily, driving the breath from his body. He rolled over, stabbing his feet into the earth to stop himself. The rifle crashed again. Dust spurted uncomfortably close to his head. He relaxed letting himself roll towards a large boulder. Rifle bullets whined around him, one sending a burning sensation across his shoulder as it drew blood. He steadied his downward roll then twisted sharply behind the boulder. Under its protection he lay panting, as the dust settled. Bullets came fast, ricocheting off the rock.

Cap cursed himself for his carelessness. A look-out must have been posted by the fencing party. He should have realized that when he saw four men riding away. But that ride had been kept casual to fool him and he had ridden into a trap with near disastrous consequences. Now he was pinned down until the rifleman decided otherwise.

Two more shots then stillness. The man must be reloading. Cap peered round the boulder cautiously but there was nothing to betray the whereabouts of the man with the rifle. Cap sank back behind the boulder, his mind working fiercely to try to find some way to get on to the trail of the riders.

He looked for his horse. The animal stood beside the water looking no worse for its fall. He weighed up the possibility of making a dash for it but there was no cover. He would be an easy target. As if the rifle-man read his thoughts and wanted to warn him against the risk, two bullets hit the ground against the boulder.

Two more shots followed. Cap tensed himself. This coyote was really going to keep him pinned down. Cap started. The last two shots had not been at him. No bullet had clipped the boulder or struck the ground nor whined close by. What the...? Then Cap saw the marksman's intention, for his horse was running further away along the river bank. Cap cursed. His lips set in a grim line. He had lost the chance of getting a lead on the fencers.

The moments seemed endless under the glare of the sun. Only the murmur of the river broke the charged silence which had settled over the scene like a clamp of doom. Irritated by his forced inactivity Cap waited to break it. No more shots came. What was happening? Dare he attempt to move from his cover? But what for? He would only make himself an easier target. He had less chance now of reaching his horse before the rifleman drew a line on him.

Suddenly Cap stiffened. The sound of a horse moving into a gallop brought him whirling to his feet. A rider broke the top of the slope some distance downstream and headed in the direction taken by the earlier riders.

The muscles twitched beside Cap's tightened jaw. He'd been outsmarted. The rifleman had moved quietly beyond the rise until he was well clear of any possible retaliatory shot from Cap.

Cap hurried to his horse but by the time he reached it the rider had long since disappeared.

Cap climbed into the saddle and rode to the top of the river-bank. He was about to set the animal for the Circle T when he checked his action. He turned the horse and sent it quickly in the direction of Jim Dixon's Lazy Y. Maybe he could still salvage something from this mess.

Cap rode fast and the thunder of the earth-tearing hooves brought curious cowboys from the Lazy Y bunk-house, from the stable and from those working some horses in the nearby corrals.

As Cap hauled his horse to a dust-stirring stop, a broad-shouldered, rugged man stepped away from the corral fence.

'You're in a mighty hurry.' There was a touch of suspicion in the man's voice.

'Yeah. Jim Dixon around?' asked Cap.

'No.'

'Who're you?'

'Who wants to know?'

Thrust and parry of the questions had brought a tension to the atmosphere. Cap was aware that the Lazy Y men had moved a step or two nearer to him and were alert to any move he might make. He would have to be quicker than they could be.

'Cap Millet,' he replied swinging out of the saddle.

'The fella I hear interrupted Mr Dixon by the river a couple of days ago!'

'The same. Who're you?'

'Walt Morgan,' answered the man.

'Foreman?' asked Cap.

'Yeah.'

'Good. As Dixon isn't here, you can tell me if five of your men have ridden in a short time ago.'

'No,' replied Walt. 'Why?'

'Let me look in your stable,' said Cap. Knowing that this request amounted to doubting the foreman's word and would get a refusal, he drew his Colt as he spoke.

Walt started. His eyes narrowed. 'Damn you, what the hell do you want?'

'First, tell your men to hold off or you'll get the first bullet,' rapped Cap, aware that his draw had intensified the tension and that men would be weighing up the chances of gunning him down without harm coming to their foreman. Walt hesitated, eyeing Cap coldly. 'Tell 'em!' Cap's voice carried an unspoken threat which he would not hesitate to carry out.

Morgan licked his lips, then raised his voice. 'Hold off!'

'Right. The stable,' said Cap as he stepped close to the foreman. With Cap's Colt menacing, the two men walked to the stables watched by the Lazy Y riders who would have cut Cap down if they'd had half a chance.

Morgan and Cap stepped into the stable. They walked the length of the building where the smell of horses permeated the air. By the time they had returned to the door Cap was puzzled. Not one of the horses showed signs of having been recently ridden.

'Satisfied?' sneered Morgan.

'How many men with Dixon?' asked Cap.

'None.'

'Right. Outside.'

They stepped into the glaring sunlight and Cap jabbed his Colt into the foreman's side as a signal to stop. The cowboys had grouped before the door but, with four strategically placed to either side, Cap realized that it only needed one chink in his vigilance or a sign from Walt and they would not hesitate to gun him down, no matter what the consequences were to themselves.

'You,' rapped Cap at the nearest man. 'How many men with Dixon?'

'None.' The reply came automatically, confirming that the foreman had spoken the truth.

'All hands here?'

The sharpness of Cap's query once again brought an immediate automatic answer. 'Yes.'

Cap was perplexed. He had felt certain that he would find horses and men showing signs of a recent hard ride but there were none.

His hesitation brought a reaction from Morgan. 'Satisfied?' he asked and when Cap did not reply added, 'What the hell's this all about?'

'I interrupted four men fencing with barbed by the river. Where Sam Grinley saw Dixon. A fifth kept me pinned down while the others rode off.'

'You figured they were Lazy Y riders,' commented Morgan. 'Well they ain't. So I suggest you put that Colt away and ride out of here mighty quick before I turn this lot on you.'

It was a serious-faced Cap who, once his Colt was back in its leather, climbed on to his horse and sent it into a quick run away from the ranch and the men who itched to get their hands on him.

SEVEN

'You all right, Sam?' Kate looked into the bedroom for the fourth time that morning.

'Yes, Ma.'

'Anything you want?'

'No, thanks.'

'I should go into town for some supplies, will you be all right if Abbe comes with me?'

'Sure, Ma.'

'You certain now?'

'Yes,' Sam turned his head to reassure his mother as she came to the bed. 'You both go. I'll be all right.'

Kate bent and kissed her son gently on the forehead. 'We won't be long, then we'll get you up.'

Sam smiled. 'Looking forward to that. Bring me some candy please.'

'Sure will,' grinned Kate, realizing in Sam's request that he was feeling much better. His passion for candy had not been spoiled.

''Bye, Sam,' Abbe called from the bedroom door ten minutes later when Kate pulled up the buggy in front of the veranda.

Sam listened to the creaks and rattles of the buggy and the clop of the horse's hooves getting fainter and fainter until they were gone completely. He bit his lip holding back the frustration which threatened to flow into self-pity. Damn it. He should have been going with them, or riding with Cap. He thumped his pillow in annoyance. Here he was face downwards in bed, his back sore and all because of Jim Dixon. Blast him. That's just what he did want – blasting. Blasting with a bullet, the murdering coyote! Sam's lips tightened at the thought. If only he'd used a cool head when he'd come across Dixon and his men, instead he'd blundered right in on them. Fool! He'd get Dixon. That was for certain. His father had taught him to use a rifle, well, one day he'd get Dixon in its sight and – bang! Dixon no more.

'Sure, Pa. I'll get him.' Sam's lips moved with silent words. 'Just for you. I will.' Sam moved his arms as if he was holding a rifle. He squinted along an imaginary barrel and followed an imaginary Dixon until the make-believe trigger was pulled sending a make-believe bullet with exceptional accuracy right into the target. 'Got you, you bastard! Got you!' Sam grinned. 'It'll be just like that, Pa, just like that. For you.'

After the excitement of the imaginary kill, Sam's mind took on a cool clinical look at the position. Get Dixon, get him now! The thought bore deeper and deeper into Sam's mind. Why not? You can do it. Do it. Do it! Sam's body tensed into a gripping excitement. He narrowed his eyes. He was looking along the rifle again. Dixon moved into the sights. He followed him. Cool. Calculating. I can do it. Yes. Kill Dixon. Kill him. Sam's mind pounded. He brushed the sweat from his forehead. The palms of his hands were clammy. He wiped them across his pillow.

Now! Go now. You'll never have another chance like this. Ma and Abbe gone to town. Cap away. You can get up. You were going to later on when ma got back. So why not now? Come on! Then you can get pa's rifle, the one he taught you to use. Then a horse. Dixon's place. Wait for him. Bang!

It was there, formed in Sam's mind. It gripped with its excitement and fulfilment of revenge. He eased himself off the bed until he was able to kneel on the floor. He pulled himself upright, the movement pulling at the wounds across his back, sending hurt through his nerves. He steadied himself against the bed and breathed deeply, fighting the pain which threatened to take over.

His mind raced. He'd never do it. He'd never make it. Sure you will. Come on. It's for pa. And for what Dixon did to you. You wouldn't be struggling like this if it hadn't been for him. You can do it.

Sam clenched his teeth as he fought against the weakness which had come to his legs. He forced himself across the room to the chair on which his shirt lay. This was going to be painful, a shirt on his back. The movements to shrug himself into his shirt aggravated the sores until Sam was sweating with the effort. His trousers and boots caused him less trouble and once he was dressed he sat for a few moments, drawing strength back into himself, preparing for the effort of getting to the stable and saddling a horse.

Ready, he got up and left his bedroom. He found his father's rifle, checked it for ammunition, picked up his Stetson and left the house.

Each step sent its own torture across his back but he fought every one. He almost succumbed to the agony to which saddling the horse subjected his body. The effort made his back scream out with the torture it felt, and his torn wrists tried to give up the weight inflicted on them when he lifted the saddle. But determination and sheer grit, coupled with the thought of Dixon in the rifle sights, drove him on to overcome the desire to soothe the hurt away.

The task completed he shoved the rifle into its scabbard and led the horse outside. He paused for a moment, leaning against the animal drawing a new energy into himself for the next step on the trail to his appointment with death.

Ready, he got his left foot into the stirrup and with a struggle which pained every fibre of his back he hauled himself up into the saddle. He sat for a few moments slumped forward, fighting the nausea which threatened to flood his mind and sap all his strength. Then, drawing deep on his reserve of will power, he sent the animal away and turned it in the direction of Dixon's Lazy Y.

Sharpening his thoughts he used the ride to renew his determination to see this through successfully and to rekindle the strength he needed to succeed against the pain which wanted to swamp him.

By the time he was nearing the Lazy Y, he had formulated his plan. He figured a position on the slight rise which ran a short distance away from one end of the house would give him a vantage point from which he could get a shot at Dixon when the rancher left the house. Accordingly he circled away from the rear of the house and came towards the edge of the rise. Judging the distance so his horse would not break the skyline he stopped the animal and slipped from its back. He drew the rifle from its leather, checked it and moved at a crouch towards the edge of the rise. All recognition of the hurtful sores across his back was gone as he concentrated on the objective of his ride. He sank to his stomach and crawled the last few yards.

Reaching the edge of the rise he surveyed the ranch-house and then the ground around him. The distance? Fine. I can do it. That hollow just to the right will give me a better position. His eyes went back to the area around the house. Some of the hands were working horses in one of the nearby corrals and two men were just going into the bunk-house. Sam inched his way to the hollow and settled down to await a sight of Dixon.

Ten minutes later, Sam was alerted by the sound of a hard-ridden horse approaching the Lazy Y. He saw that the pounding hooves had drawn the curiosity of the Lazy Y hands. Maybe Dixon would come out of the house. Sam settled himself with an empty feeling gripping the pit of his stomach. He felt his hands tremble as he positioned the rifle. This won't do. Get a hold of yourself. Relax. Sam forced the tension out of himself. Dixon? He'd have been out by now if he was in the house. Sam glanced at the rider. For a moment he didn't believe his eyes. Cap! What the hell was he doing here? Curious, Sam riveted all his attention on the scene below him trying to figure out the reasons behind Cap taking Walt Morgan to the stable at gun point to emerge a short while later and ride off. Sam could find no answers and finally dismissed the whole business from his mind to prime himself for his purpose.

Half an hour passed when another rider drew his attention. He was approaching the ranch at a leisurely pace and it was a little while before Sam recognized Jim Dixon. Dixon! A shiver ran through him. Dixon was back. Sam licked his lips and swallowed hard. This was it. The revenge which had burned inside him seemed to have paled. He was faced with the job he had set himself – to kill. But could he? Could he kill a man?

'Damn you, Sam, damn you.' His lips

quivered as he spoke to himself in a low voice, trying to steel himself to the task, forcing the resolve firmly back into his mind, excluding everything else. 'Sure you can do it. You're chickening? You're a man now Dixon saw to that. So you treat him as a man.'

Sam pulled a handkerchief from his pocket. He wiped the sweat from his forehead and dabbed the droplets from his lips. He stared hard at Dixon. Get ready, or you'll let the opportunity go. Sam rubbed his hands on the handkerchief and stuffed it back into his pocket quickly. The sharpness of the movement seemed to restrengthen his resolve. He grasped the rifle firmly and drew a line on Dixon as he rode nearer and nearer the buildings.

The sighting blurred. Sam knuckled his eyes, blinked and sighted again. Clear. His arms began to tremble. He eased them, took a deep breath and steadied himself.

'Calm yourself, Sam. Relax. Easy now.' He could hear his father's words. He repeated them over and over to himself as he kept a line on Dixon.

The rider paused. Spoke to Walt Morgan. Watched the men working the horses in the corral for a few moments.

'Come on, come on,' Sam whispered to himself. 'Steady now, keep calm. He'll come. Be patient.'

He felt the sun pouring through his shirt, burning at the sores, reminding of the objective he had set himself. He must not fail.

Dixon put his horse into a walk again after a final word to Walt Morgan. He neared the house. Called to one of the men who came running.

'Now, Sam, now. Don't wait. He'll be off the horse and into the house soon.' Sam licked his lips. Relined his sighting. Everything else faded from his vision as his concentration was directed at Jim Dixon. Perfect. Perfect. Gently, now, gently. Don't pull, just squeeze lightly. Now!

A rifle crashed across the quiet, work-a-day scene.

Sam saw Jim Dixon jerk. He seemed to freeze for one moment in the saddle and then slowly tumble sideways to crash heavily to the ground and lie still. The whole scene froze before his eyes, printing itself indelibly on his mind.

Then suddenly, as if released, it burst into movement as men raced to the owner of the Lazy Y.

143

Sam started, the numbness which had gripped him banished with the realization that Dixon had been hit and showed no sign of movement. He'd done it! He'd revenged his father! He'd made Dixon pay! He'd done... Sam's mind exploded. He looked down at his finger still on the trigger. His eyes widened with disbelief. He hadn't squeezed the trigger! But Dixon... Sam glanced up sharply, his eyes piercing the distance to check that they had not deceived him. They hadn't, they were right. Dixon had been shot! But how? Who? Sam's thoughts tumbled, chasing each other as they sought answers.

The pandemonium, which had erupted on the Lazy Y, had been brought under control by Walt Morgan. Men were pointing beyond the ranch in the opposite direction to Sam. Others were running for their horses and once in the saddle sent their mounts in pursuit of the unseen assassin.

Sam stiffened. It could have been him. What would he have done? He had made no plans for escape. He relaxed with some relief as he realized the dilemma from which he had been saved. Instead of the anxiety of escaping capture he could ride calmly home instead. Even as he drew comfort from these thoughts a new dilemma seized him. He'd uttered threats at Dixon. He'd been heard by the marshal and by some of Dixon's men. If the killer wasn't caught he'd be a suspect! Panic began to take hold of his mind. They'd come for him. They'd want to know where he'd been. They'd find out! Sam stiffened with horror. This was something he hadn't thought about. He had uttered threats so he'd be the first suspect.

He scrambled out of the hollow and crept quickly to his horse, ignoring the pain which scorched his back with every movement. Hauling himself into the saddle, he sent the animal away in a gallop. With his mind in a whirl, cool reasoning had vanished. He just rode with the object of getting away from the Lazy Y as quickly as possible.

Panic drove him for half an hour before his mind started to clear and warned him to remove the desperation from his ride. He slowed the horse and gentled it into a walking pace. He must not exhaust himself nor the animal for there was no knowing how far he would have to ride before he was safe. But where should he go? Where would he be safe from pursuit?

His mother would be home now and she would be wondering where he was. Should he go home and run the risk of being arrested? Sam licked his parched lips as he wrestled with his problems. How he wished he had a canteen of water. Water. Maybe that was the answer. Go to the place he and his father had found in the hills. There was water there. Then maybe under cover of darkness he'd be able to ride home, reassure his ma he was all right, get some food and then get clear of the district.

Sam turned his horse towards the distant hills, shimmering in the blue haze.

EIGHT

When the Lazy Y rider hit town, the news of Jim Dixon's murder spread like a prairie fire. A crowd clamoured around the marshal's office while, inside, the rider gave the facts quickly to Clint Holmes and his deputy, Bert Shelldon.

The lawmen were strapping on their gunbelts when the door opened and the huge bulk of Matt Westwood strode in.

'What the hell happened?' he asked.

'Jim shot by an unseen rifleman,' rapped Clint tersely.

'Where?'

'At the ranch.'

'Anyone get after him?'

'Sure,' replied the man from the Lazy Y, 'but I figure he'd be long gone before our boys were saddled up.'

'You raising a posse?' asked Westwood, swinging his gaze back to the marshal.

'I reckon I can raise the Lazy Y boys to ride with me,' replied Clint, as he grabbed his Stetson.

'Couple of my hands outside, they can ride with you,' offered Westwood.

'All right,' called Holmes over his shoulder as he reached the door.

The lawmen hurried out followed by the Lazy Y rider. As they went to their horses, they ignored the questions flung at them from various sections of the milling crowd. They climbed into the saddles and parted the folk pressing around them when they turned their mounts.

As Westwood stepped from the office on the sidewalk his sharp glance caught the attention of two men. With it there was an order which they acknowledged. A few moments later Buck Masters and Wes Dilland were putting their horses into a fast gallop chasing the dust from the hooves of the three animals ahead of them.

'Any luck?' yelled the marshal as the five riders hauled their horses to an earth-tearing halt on reaching the Lazy Y.

'None!' called back foreman, Walt Morgan.

The marshal dropped from the saddle. 'Where did the shot come from?' he asked.

'From the hillside over there.' Morgan indicated the direction. 'I figure that group of boulders.'

'And Jim was where?'

'Just over here.' Morgan led the way to the spot.

The marshal eyed it and then looked towards the hillside. He weighed up the distance with an experienced eye. 'Mighty good shot from there to kill Jim outright,' he observed.

'Any ideas? Anyone been around?' asked Clint.

'That stranger, Cap Millet, came looking for Dixon. He'd seen someone erecting barbed wire, figured they were Lazy Y men. Came here to check the stables.'

'You let him?'

'Used his gun.'

'Find anything?'

'No. All hands were here, never been away, only Mr Dixon.'

Holmes nodded thoughtfully. 'Millet stopped Jim flogging Sam Grinley I hear.'

Morgan's eyes widened as he replied, 'Yeah. Hi, that kid threatened Dixon. Figured he'd get him for killing his pa. Never reckoned on him...'

'Mighty fine shot for a kid,' remarked Clint.

'Not so much of a kid,' put in Deputy Bert Shelldon who had joined the two men. 'His pa taught him to use a rifle.'

149

'Then I figure we get after him,' urged Morgan. 'He's made the threats and…'

'All right, let's get to the Circle T,' agreed Clint.

Morgan yelled to his riders, delegating three Lazy Y riders, as well as himself, to make up the posse.

In a matter of moments the eight riders, closely bunched, headed for the Circle T in a determined ride which boded ill for the killer of Jim Dixon.

'Ma, can I take Sam his candy?' cried Abbe excitedly as her mother brought the buggy to a stop outside the house.

'Surely,' agreed Kate with a smile.

Abbe turned round, grabbed the bag from the basket resting on the floor of the buggy and jumped down. Kate watched her daughter leap up the steps and race into the house. What small things excited Abbe. This time it was the fact that they were bringing Sam twice as much candy as he would be expecting.

Kate stepped down from the buggy and tied the horse to the rail. She was reaching for the basket when the door of the house crashed open.

'Ma! Ma!' The frightened panic in Abbe's

voice brought Kate spinning round in alarm.

'Abbe, what is it?' she gasped, seeing the bewilderment in Abbe's face which had been drained of its colour.

'Ma! Sam's not there!' cried Abbe as she flung herself down the steps.

'What!'

'He's not there!'

Kate stared at the door of the house with disbelief as she started forward. Abbe turned beside her and Kate's arm automatically came round her shoulders as if to protect the girl from the unknown. Fear gripped Kate as she raced into the house.

'Sam! Sam!' She tore the bedroom door open. No one. All the bedclothes flung back, Sam's shirt, trousers, boots, gone. With Abbe following close behind, Kate ran to the other two bedrooms and then into the kitchen. No one. She flung open the back door. 'Sam! Sam! You there?' But no answer came from the privy.

Her son gone, vanished. It seemed impossible. Kate turned slowly from the door but her mind was racing through the possibilities for Sam's disappearance.

'Where can he be, Ma?' asked Abbe still clutching the bag of candy.

'I wish I knew,' sighed Kate. Suddenly she turned. 'The stable!'

Mother and daughter ran from the house and, gasping for breath, entered the stable. No one. A horse missing.

Kate eyed the empty stall as despair filled her heart. 'Oh! No!' she moaned.

Fearing the worst she hurried back to the house. She stopped in her step when she went inside and stared at the empty corner. Joe's rifle gone! Cold fingers clutched at her heart. The colour drained from her face.

'Oh, Sam!' The words came in a long drawn-out whisper of dejection as she sank to a chair.

'Ma, what is it?' asked Abbe, alarm widening her eyes.

'Your pa's rifle's gone,' whispered Kate still staring at the corner where it had stood.

'Sam taken it?'

'Must have.' Kate glanced at Abbe and added quickly before the girl could ask any more questions. 'Bring the things in from the buggy please.'

As Abbe went outside, Kate leaned back in the chair with a deep sigh which seemed to drain all the life from her. The weight of the problem seemed oppressive. What could she do? If only there was someone to turn to. If only Cap was here.

She could ride to the Lazy Y, warn Dixon. She started to get off the chair when Abbe came in and carried the basket through to the kitchen. Warn Dixon. She sank back again. That would not do. Warning Dixon would only set up a death-trap for Sam.

Kate bit her lip, fighting back the tears which threatened to come. She must not let Abbe see her like this. Abbe hurried out to the buggy again and when she returned with a box of goods her mother was busy unpacking the basket.

Kate continued to try to occupy herself in spite of her demented state of mind. How long she carried on in this way she never knew but in the midst of washing-up the cups they had used for some tea, the intrusion of an approaching horse sent her rushing hopefully on to the veranda.

'Is it Sam?' cried Abbe as she ran after her mother.

Kate's hopes crashed when she saw the rider was Cap. Sam, oh why wasn't it Sam? Tears welled in her eyes. It should have been Sam. But it was Cap and now she would not be alone with her problem.

She stood at the top of the steps nervously awaiting his arrival.

'Abbe, go and get some coffee on,' she said quickly when Cap drew near.

As Cap stopped his horse he realized something was wrong. Kate answered his query before the words came to his lips.

'Sam's gone!'

'What!' Cap stared incredulously at Kate for a moment then was quickly out of the saddle and beside her on the veranda.

'He's taken Joe's rifle!' the possible implications choked the words in Kate's throat.

'My God!' gasped Cap. 'And he threatened Dixon.'

'Yes.' Kate's eyes widened. 'What are we going to do?'

'I was at Dixon's earlier, he wasn't there. If I get back quickly there may be just a chance.'

'You were there? Why?' Kate's queries halted Cap's move to his horse.

'Saw some men fencing. Got pinned down by a rifle while they got away. Figured they might be Lazy Y men so rode there to check it out.'

'Were they?'

Cap shook his head. 'No. I'm puzzled by it all. Foreman swore Dixon was the only man not at the ranch. I checked it out, he was telling the truth.'

'If that's so Dixon may not be behind the fencing.'

'And that might mean he had nothing to do with Joe's death, like he says.'

'Oh, my God!' gasped Kate, a sickening feeling hitting her stomach, 'and Sam has Joe's rifle.'

'I'll get back to the Lazy Y as quick as I can.' Cap turned but froze to the spot.

A band of horsemen were riding towards the ranch. They were bunched with an air of determined purpose about them. Eight men weren't merely paying a courtesy call.

'A posse!' gasped Kate, with the fear of its meaning welling inside her.

Cap nodded.

'Sam! Oh, no! He can't…' Kate's voice trailed away, the words lost in the tumbling confusion of thoughts which flooded her mind.

'Steady,' said Cap comfortingly. 'Let's hear what they have to say first.'

The horses sent dust billowing from their hooves as they approached the house and were brought to a controlled stop by their grim-faced riders.

'Howdy, ma'm,' greeted Marshal Holmes touching the brim of his Stetson and edging his horse a little nearer. He gave Cap a brief nod of recognition. 'I'm sorry to trouble you, ma'm,' the lawman went on directing his gaze at Kate. 'Can I have a word with Sam?'

Kate's immediate instinct was to protect her son, say he was too ill to see anyone but she knew it would be useless. She would not be able to disguise the agitation, the nervousness and these men would guess she was lying. The marshal would use his power to search the house. Nevertheless Kate automatically stalled for time.

'What do you want him for?' she asked.

'Jim Dixon's been shot dead,' replied Holmes.

'Oh no!' The thing which she had dreaded since finding Joe's rifle missing was overwhelming her. 'No, not Sam!'

The marshal noted the surprise over Cap's face at the news and reckoned that Cap did not know about the killing or was a damned good actor.

'You sure it was Sam?' Cap asked.

'No,' replied Holmes.

'Nobody saw the killer?' pressed Cap.

'No,' clipped Holmes, irritated by the questioning when he should be doing the enquiring.

'Then why you looking for Sam?' asked Kate.

'Just checking, ma'm,' replied Holmes. 'After all, Sam did threaten Dixon after Joe was killed, and from what I hear he has other reasons.'

'Hell, marshal, Sam was in no fit state to go after Dixon,' rapped Cap.

'Surprising how desire for revenge can drive a man if the opportunity arises. You two can't be around all the time to keep an eye on him.' The protests which sprang to Kate's lips were left unspoken as the marshal went on. 'You were seen in town, m'am. And you,' he eyed Cap, 'were at the Lazy Y. I checked the times. Sam would be here on his own.' His eyes narrowed. 'Could be you doubled back and shot Dixon, Millet!'

Cap stiffened at the accusation. His lips tightened as he spat back. 'Take me in if you figure that.'

The marshal ignored the remark and turned his attention back to Kate. 'Know where Sam might be?' he asked.

'No.' Kate shook her head as the word choked in her throat.

The marshal nodded. 'Thanks, m'am. We'll continue looking.' He turned his horse and, followed by the grim-faced, silent posse, rode away.

Kate, her body numb, her mind in a tumble at the thought of her son being hunted by a posse of men, watched until startled by Cap's voice.

'Kate,' he said gently, sorry to bring her back from the world of disbelief to face reality.

She swung round her eyes widening with fear. 'They're going to kill him!' she cried.

'Easy now,' soothed Cap. 'The marshal won't let that happen.'

'But didn't you see it?' Kate's voice rose shrilly matching the wildness which came to her eyes with Cap's apparent casualness. 'It was in their eyes. Dixon's men will do it. They'll find the excuse.'

Cap knew it was no use trying to fool Kate. She had seen too much roughness and violence in the settlement of a land where the law was not always impartial. 'Yes, Kate, I saw it,' he said. This confirmation seemed to bring some relief to Kate and, as Cap went on, she saw some hope in spite of the odds stacked against them. 'I've got to find Sam first!'

The light of new hope which came to her eyes faded with the doubt she voiced, 'But how? Where?'

'That's what I hoped you'd be able to tell me,' replied Cap.

'Me? How could I know? Sam had gone when we got back from town.' Kate was puzzled. 'Hadn't he, Abbe?' She sank wearily on to a chair.

Abbe who had been bewildered by the whole affair hastened to confirm her mother's statement.

'I know. I wasn't implying that you were in cahoots with Sam,' said Cap. 'But you might be able to tell me where I can find him. Sit down and tell me all you can about Sam, where he used to go, what he used to do.' Cap paused a moment and then, as he looked seriously at Kate, he went on. 'We must, at this stage, assume that Sam killed Dixon.' The look of angry protest which came to Kate's face made Cap hasten to reassure her. 'I'm not saying he did, but if we don't assume that he did your thinking may not go along the right lines. If Sam killed Dixon he wouldn't come back here, so where would he go?'

With anguish replacing the anger, Kate bit her lips in frustration as her mind raced to latch on to something which might help. 'Oh, I don't know,' she cried in despair. Lines etched deep into her face with the problem.

'Think, Kate,' pressed Cap. 'What did he use to do as a kid? Any special places he'd go to?'

Kate shook her head. 'He was around the ranch mostly.'

'Mostly,' said Cap. 'What about the rest of the time?'

'Town,' Kate's thoughts deepened the furrows in her forehead. 'Fishing. Go off down to the river, maybe away all day,' she mused recalling the past.

'That doesn't help much,' said Cap. 'No leads there. Sam's not likely to go to town and the river offers no place to hide.' He looked anxiously at Kate, willing her to remember something else.

She caught the urgency in his eyes but shook her head.

'When he went off with his pa was it working?' pressed Cap.

'Mm.' A flash of recall scorched her mind. 'There were times when they returned and I'd ask them where they'd been, they'd say the hill country.' She paused deep in thought then suddenly banged her knee with her clenched fist in exasperation. 'If only I could remember. There's something jingling in the back of my mind.' Her lips tightened with the frustration.

160

'Ma. They found that little valley,' broke in Abbe.

Kate sat bolt upright. Her eyes danced with excitement. 'That's right, Abbe, they did. A couple of years ago.' She turned to Cap. 'That might be it. Sam might have gone there!'

Cap smiled reassuringly at Kate. 'Could be. Sounds as though no one else knew about it.'

'Not as far as I know,' confirmed Kate.

'It was a secret.' Abbe exploded with excitement at the realization that she had contributed something of probable importance. 'Sam told me no one else knew.'

'Probably just boy talk,' Kate pointed out to Cap.

'No, Ma. It was true,' went on Abbe. 'Sam said he'd take me there one day when I was older.'

'Did he take you there?' asked Cap eagerly.

'Not yet,' replied Abbe.

'So you don't know where it is?' pressed Cap.

'In the hills,' answered Abbe.

'Where exactly?'

Abbe looked glum and shook her head. Disappointed that the excitement had been muted, that maybe she hadn't contributed much after all, brought a tear to overflow and run down her cheek.

'That's all right,' comforted Cap, patting her arm. 'You've been a great help. Don't worry. I'll find it.'

There were thanks and hope in her own smile as she rubbed the tears away.

Cap glanced at Kate an unspoken question in his eyes.

Kate shook her head. 'No, I don't know where it is.'

'Not a clue? Just one clue to point me in the right direction once I get in the hills?' Cap urged Kate to drag the depths of her mind.

She rubbed her hand wearily across her face. 'No,' she replied. She repeated the word only this time it was drawn out as if doubting it was the right answer. 'Wait a moment. Something's coming.' Her excitement enveloped both Cap and Abbe. 'Joe said something about a cleft in a wall of rock. They'd come on it by sheer chance.'

'Good, good,' cried Cap eagerly, wanting Kate to go on. 'That could narrow the search. Must be a rougher section of the hill country.'

'There is,' went on Kate enthusiastically.

'Towards the northwest corner the hills are much more rugged, more bare rock, the valleys tend to be deeper and narrower.' She paused, but it was only for the briefest of moments. In that split second of time a new excitement danced into her eyes. 'Eagle Rock! I heard Joe and Sam talking one day. Said Eagle Rock would always be a marker.'

'Do you know where it is?' urged Cap.

'No, but it must be in those hills.' Kate's excitement began to fade as doubts came to her and she tentatively put the question, 'Mustn't it?'

'More than likely,' said Cap with some enthusiasm to restore Kate's flagging spirit. 'One more thing,' his voice took on a more serious tone, matching the expression on his face. 'Give me a run down on the men who rode with the sheriff and his deputy.'

Kate glanced curiously at Cap but did not query why he wanted that information.

'Four of Dixon's men including the foreman Walt Morgan.'

'That figures. The other two?'

'New riders for Westwood. Buck Masters and Wes Dilland,' replied Kate.

'Ma, I saw them talking to Mr Westwood when we were in town,' said Abbe.

'You sure?' asked Cap.

163

'Yes,' replied Abbe firmly.

'Thanks,' said Cap. 'That may be very useful.'

'How?' queried Kate.

'Figure it this way. If Sam didn't kill Dixon, whom he suspected had killed his father, then someone who knew about Sam's threat killed Dixon hoping to put the blame on Sam.'

'But why? Do you think that whoever killed Dixon killed Joe?' queried Kate.

'Could be. Someone wanted Joe and Dixon out of the way. As far as I can see the only reason is this land, wanting to fence a big area before homesteaders arrive in numbers. Joe was killed after an argument with Dixon. Someone who knew about that argument, saw the chance of getting the Circle T by getting rid of Joe and putting the blame on Dixon. With Dixon convicted the men behind the killings could move in on the Lazy Y.'

The realization about what Cap was getting at came slowly to Kate. 'But then I said we weren't moving, we were going to run the Circle T.'

'Right,' agreed Cap.

'But I told that to only one person,' said Kate.

'You sure?' Cap pressed for certainty.

'Definitely. Matt Westwood after the funeral.'

'Right. You refused him so both ranches are still occupied. Westwood knows of Sam threatening Dixon so switches tactics, kills Dixon and Sam gets the blame.'

'And with Sam caught or killed resisting arrest both ranches are vacant,' whispered Kate incredulously.

'It's the only way I can figure it,' confirmed Cap. 'Seemed to click into place when Abbe mentioned those two men talking to Westwood.'

'My God, they're riding with posse!' cried Kate, the horror of the possibilities flooding into her mind.

NINE

Once over the rise a mile beyond the Circle T ranch-house Marshal Clint Holmes called his posse to a halt.

'Anyone figure anything from that encounter?' he asked casting his eye around the group, posing his question again silently as his firm gaze met each man in turn.

'Only that we ain't no nearer getting a lead on Sam Grinley,' muttered Walt Morgan.

'Right,' agreed Clint. 'So we split forces here. We concluded that Sam had done the shooting and came straight to the Circle T. We never tried to pick up his trail back at the Lazy Y. Bert,' he turned to his deputy, 'you take the Lazy Y boys and go try to pick up a trail. I figure that Cap Millet may know more about this and may try to contact Sam. I'll stay here and keep tabs on Millet.' He glanced at the other two men. 'You're free to return to the Running W and thank Matt Westwood for letting you ride with me.'

'We'll hang on with you,' replied the

167

shorter, stockier man whose dark eyes sought approval from his companion. 'Wes?'

'Sure will, Buck,' replied Wes easing his willowy frame in the saddle. 'Mister Westwood would want us to help all we can. Who knows, he might be the next target.'

'Right,' said Clint. 'Glad to have you.'

As the deputy marshal led the Lazy Y cowboys away, Clint extracted his spy-glass from its leather, slipped from the saddle and, with Wes and Buck, positioned himself so that they could watch the Circle T ranch-house.

Clint was beginning to feel uneasy and conclude that his supposition had been wrong when, after an hour, Cap had not appeared.

'Like a long cool beer?' asked Buck with a grin as Clint wiped the sweat from his face.

'It's blasted hot out here. Ain't Millet going to move?' snapped Clint irritably.

'Say, why don't we ride in there and make him talk?' suggested Wes, cracking the knuckles of his right hand at the thought of beating someone up.

'Figure you'd make Millet talk?' said Clint, a note of doubt in his voice. 'I reckon he ain't that sort.'

'You ain't seen Wes at work,' grinned Buck.

'There's a woman in the house.' Wes's hard laugh revealed the pleasure he would get in making Cap talk.

Clint frowned. 'That ain't the way of the law,' he snapped. He wasn't too sure of these latest additions to the Running W. They had been with Westwood a month but had given the law no cause to run against them. They had been involved with running some homesteaders off the range and rumour had it that they'd been a bit rough on some of the women folk. But the law in cattlemen's country sometimes had to turn a blind eye.

'Sorry, Marshal.' Wes made a mock apology. 'Thought maybe you'd let us get on with the job instead of hanging around in this damned heat. No need for you to be there.'

Clint scowled but made no reply. He raised his spy-glass to his eye and surveyed the ranch-house again. Still no movement.

Suddenly he stiffened. 'Something happening!' He saw Kate and Abbe come out followed by Cap. They came down the veranda steps to Cap's horse. He took some packages they were carrying and put them in his saddle-bags. 'Supplies,' muttered Clint. 'Figure we're on to something.' He watched Cap swing into the saddle, pause and say something to Kate and Abbe before riding off.

They watched him head in their direction and then after half a mile turn towards the hills.

'This is it!' said Clint with excitement in his voice. 'The hill country. Plenty of hiding-places there. And as I figure Millet knew more than he admitted.' He grinned at Wes and Buck. 'We've got him!'

They watched Cap until it was safe for them to slip on to his trail without betraying their presence.

The hills. Sam welcomed them as his horse moved steadily onward. At least here there was more cover. The ride across the open grassland had been filled with anxiety. Many an anxious glance had been cast behind him but not one had revealed pursuit. Now he had a better chance of escape. And once he reached that secret valley, which only he and his father had shared, he'd be safe. A perfect hide-out. He'd wait there until he figured things had quietened down and then he'd slip home under the cover of darkness, get supplies, reassure his ma and find a new life somewhere else.

His throat constricted. He swallowed hard, choking back the gnawing ache in his stomach. A new life. Why? He hadn't done anything. He hadn't shot Dixon. But who would believe him? He'd threatened. He'd had cause. Now he was an outcast, a fugitive from the law. A fugitive! Me! Why me! Tears brimmed in his eyes. His back hurt. The sun seared it into sharper pain. Ma! If only... He licked at his parched lips. Water. He needed water. He'd find some in his valley. There he'd be safe. He urged his horse on.

He felt tired, weary. The effort of the ride, the tension of waiting and watching for Dixon had all taken their toll on a body weakened by the beating it had taken. And he had achieved nothing. He had gained no satisfaction of revenge. But who had killed Dixon? Why? Sam's thoughts were a maze of confusion as he rode deeper and deeper into the hills.

The land began to grow rough. The hills were less rounded and began to take on a more jagged appearance. He stopped his horse more frequently to reassess his bearings, shielding his eyes against the searing brightness of the sky as he searched for guiding landmarks.

The hills were lifting and closing around

him. Sweat poured from his body. He breathed deeply, trying to find strength to carry on but even the air seemed to stifle instead of renewing. He removed his battered Stetson, wiped his face with his forearm, sighed and squinted his eyes as he stared upwards at the barren hillsides.

Tension gripped him. Excitement fought the gnawing anxiety in his stomach. Yes, there it was! Eagle Rock! It faded. He blinked. It wasn't there. Sam cursed loudly, decrying the heavens for playing tricks on him. It was there. It must be. He knuckled the dampness of frustration from his eyes. Yes! Eagle Rock! It stood out clear, sharp in silhouette against the bright sky. Excitement seized him once again. The next valley. Then his own.

He tapped his horse forward. A quarter of a mile and he turned into a narrow valley where, after half a mile, the barren hillsides steepened into perpendicular walls of rock. Sam moved closer and closer to the right-hand side of the valley. He rode slowly, allowing his eyes time to search every inch of the brown-grey rock.

The minutes ticked away. Sam grew anxious. Had he missed it? No, surely not. He shuddered in the gloom cast by the

172

towering hill. Suddenly he felt terribly lonely. How he wished it was the last time he had been here. His father had been with him. He had need of him now.

His eyes strained, searching, searching. There it is! He stopped his horse. Is it? Is that dark patch the cleft he sought? He turned his horse towards it. The blackness cut back into the rock. Trying to ignore the hurt in his back, which screwed up his face, he slipped off the saddle. He moved towards the cut and saw it was nothing more. An aching disappointment seized him as he stepped back to his horse and picked up the reins. He led the horse as he moved closer to the rock face.

There! This cut into the rock was wider. This must be it. He led the animal in to the gap. The horse whinnied a protest.

'Quiet!' snapped Sam, startled by the noise. Then more gently he added, 'Come on, it's all right. Don't you remember it?'

Sam moved on, gentling the horse with soothing tones. The cleft meandered for half a mile with only a wisp of brightness high overhead to relieve the oppressive gloom of the dank rock which never felt the drying glow of the sun.

Sam shivered, uncertain as to whether he

preferred the chill, which seemed to drive to his bones, or the sun scorching the sores on his back. But the knowledge that soon he would be able to choose the shade or open sun in his valley carried him on.

After half a mile the cleft widened slowly as if it wasn't prepared to reveal all at once. Sam caught a glimpse of his valley. He pressed on eagerly. Then he was through, free of the towering walls of rock. Before him lay an open space about a mile long and half a mile wide. Rocks lowered on either side but at the opposite end they rose more gently towards a final hundred feet of precipitous rock. A stream tumbled into the valley and flowed its length before disappearing underground.

Sam's heart raced. He felt something of the load lifted from his shoulders. He was safe! No one would find him here. He patted his horse's neck comfortingly then swung into the saddle. The animal moved forward and Sam guided it until he found a suitable place to bed down near the stream.

Slipping out of the saddle he led the horse to the water, let it have its freedom and then stretched himself full length on his stomach to slake his thirst from the crystal-clear, bouncing stream. Having drunk he dipped his head in the water, held it there, then pulled it out, blowing and sweeping the wet from his face with his hands. It felt good and drove some new life back into Sam.

He scrambled to his feet, shook the surplus water from his hair and looked around him. Selecting a suitable spot, he unsaddled his horse and placed his gear on the ground. He spread the blanket, laid his rifle on it and stretched out beside it. With relaxation came exhaustion and in a matter of moments Sam was fast asleep.

Cap kept his horse to a steady pace. He curbed his desire to hurry, to find Sam as quickly as possible, for that might take some time, might necessitate a lot of travelling for which he would need to conserve his horse's energy.

Since the possibility of contacting Sam had been raised by Abbe recalling the valley in the hills Cap had been anxious to be on his way. He was glad now that he had taken notice of Kate to wait until she had got some supplies and clothing ready. He knew she too was just as eager for him to find her son but in her practical wisdom she saw that provisions might be necessary.

Cap turned his problem over in his mind

as he rode, relaxed in the saddle. A cleft in a wall of rock leading to a secret valley. A guide in the form of a landmark known as Eagle Rock so named after an old Indian superstition. Little for a man who did not know the country to work on. But Cap was determined to succeed. He had to for Kate and Abbe and for Sam. He had to know the truth. If Sam had killed Dixon then his theories were all wrong and he did not know how he could break the news to Kate and Abbe.

Cap was well in the hills by the time the light was slipping quickly from the sky. Being unfamiliar with the country, Cap knew it would be unwise to press on. So he found a suitable place to bed down for the night. As he ate his beans and bread and drank his coffee, he wondered how Sam was faring and wished he had him here with him now.

The following morning Cap was awake early, unaware that his stirrings had taken a man scurrying back to another camp to warn his companions that Cap was on the move.

By mid-morning Cap was leaving the gentler landscape for the rougher terrain. Now his problems started. Which direction?

Which valley amongst the upheaval contained the secret, the cleft which might lead him to Sam?

He eased his horse to a halt at the top of a rise and pulled out his spy-glass. He spent half an hour studying the land ahead. A succession of valleys cut far into the country and how many more lay hidden from his view he could not tell. Any one of them might be the one he wanted. He looked to the heights. Eagle Rock? But where? From his position it was difficult to study individual shapes. He needed to be nearer to throw their silhouettes into prominence. He turned his attention back to the valleys, seeking as far as he could precipitous walls of rock.

The three nearest valleys were eliminated immediately for their sides rose in sweeping rounds. Beyond, the terrain became more rugged and Cap knew that he needed to be in that upheaval. He stowed his spyglass and put the horse into a steady, distance-consuming motion.

The sun had passed its zenith when Cap moved into a wide valley out of which a series of narrower valleys struck south. Cap hoped that one of these would prove to be the one for which he was looking but, from his position, he could see nothing which bore any resemblance to an eagle. Seeing a knoll on the north side of the valley he turned his horse towards it, hoping that it might give him a better vantage point from which to study the landscape.

Reaching the top of the knoll he halted his horse to find that the extra height enabled him to see the heights beyond the series of valleys. A number of protrusions broke the skyline. Could one of them be the landmark which might guide him to Sam? Eagerly he pulled out his spy-glass and scanned the distance quickly. Nothing resembled an eagle. Disappointment weighed heavily as Cap began a more careful study. Still nothing.

He frowned as he lowered his spy-glass. He felt he was near and yet he couldn't see the guiding landmark. Something nagged at him. He let his eyes scan the landscape again. Those protrusions of rock stood out but not one... His body went taut as other thoughts intruded and took over. Those protrusions would take on different shapes from different positions. He could be looking at Eagle Rock but not from the right place to see what its name implied. He quickly studied the position of the rocks in relation to the valleys and realized that one or more would be visible from the entrance to each valley.

Excitement, coupled with his eagerness to test his idea, tempered his urging of his horse. The animal responded and earth flew beneath its cutting hooves as it pounded down the slope and across the floor of the valley.

Cap slowed his mount as he neared the first valley. His eyes searched eagerly but only a finger of rock broke the skyline above the heights.

He sent his horse into a gallop, slowed it at the entrance of the next valley, searched without success and moved on. Despair and disappointment were creeping insidiously into his mind as he rode to the fourth valley. Half expecting to make a fruitless search again, he was already tapping his horse forward when the full impression penetrated his mind. That rock! The one which was highest in a group of three gave the impression that it was soaring above the valley. A bird! Could it be an eagle? He pulled his spyglass from its leather in feverish excitement. Focusing it, he quickly drew the rock towards him. Eagle? No doubt. The Indian legend could interpret it that way!

Cap drew his gaze downwards to search the shadows of the distant reaches of the valley. The sides narrowed towards each other as they rose into perpendicular, soaring walls of rock and curved to meet each other in the massive gloom which marked the valley's end.

Cap stowed his spyglass excitedly. This could be it! Walls of rock! Eagle Rock! He pushed his horse forward.

As he passed from view three men, anxious not to lose contact, tapped their horses into a quick run.

TEN

Cap kept to a steady pace as he rode deeper and deeper into the valley. Every nerve of his being was charged to the peak of alertness. His eyes, sharp, keen, searched the sunlit terrain and probed the shadows on the opposite side of the valley.

The further he rode the steeper the hills became until he was riding between towering walls of rock which allowed no sun to penetrate their depths. The bird-like rock which had hovered as he entered the valley, now seemed oppressive. It dominated, leering down as if seeking plunder. Now it appeared to be swooping, its curved beak ready to tear, its head held in evil gesture. No wonder the Indians held it in awe through legend. Cap cursed his imagination and forced himself to concentrate more and more on his search for the cleft he hoped would lead him to Sam.

The valley floor, strewn with rocks and boulders, rose gently for about a hundred yards before flattening, to run to the soaring rock-face which sent fingers of stone in muted adoration to its predominant pinnacle.

Cap halted his horse. He probed the left-hand mass of rock. Cuts, cracks, fissures, but nothing which would allow a horse to pass through. He turned the animal across the narrowing valley to scrutinize the right-hand side. This wall of rock appeared to be broken by gashes, as if some gigantic axe had attempted to cleave it.

Maybe here he would find what he wanted. Excited tension gripped Cap as he edged his mount closer to the rock-face. He moved slowly, examining the darker gloom carefully. Nothing. Nothing. Nothing. Every time he drew no result his mouth set deeper into a tight, grim line.

The horse's steps were slow and deliberate between each pause. Encouraged by Cap's soft, gentle voice it subdued its nervous reaction to the deepening gloom and over-bearing rock. Suddenly the animal sensed a new excitement in Cap's touch as the rider steadied it in a prolonged pause.

Cap slid from the saddle. A moment later he was stepping into a large cleft in the rock face. With only a thin strip of light high above he waited until his eyes got used to the gloom before moving forward cautiously. After about a hundred yards with no sign of the cleft coming to an end Cap decided to return for his horse. This may well be the cleft for which he had been looking and he figured it was no good having to return for his horse later. He hurried back and soon emerged into the valley to find his horse had moved a few yards away from the cleft.

'I think we might have found Sam,' he said enthusiastically as he picked up the reins and patted the horse's neck. He turned and started to lead the animal towards the cleft.

'Figure we're gettin' nearer, Marshal?' queried Buck, his dark eyes piercing from below his bushy eyebrows.

'Could be,' replied Clint. 'There's no way out of this valley.'

'Seems as though Millet knows where he's heading.'

'Not so sure,' Clint pointed out. 'He made a long survey from that knoll back yonder.'

'Wal, he chose this valley so looks as if he picked up something to guide him.'

'Whether he's right or not I'll be mighty glad to get into that shade,' said Wes as he automatically raised his bandanna to wipe the sweat and dust from his face.

Clint half turned in his saddle to add some remark but the words remained unspoken, held back by the fleetest glimpse of a mark on Wes's neck. Controlling his surprise as quickly as it came, the marshal made his turn look as if he was easing himself in his saddle.

Rope burn! The words thundered in Clint's mind. He was sure. He'd seen rope burn before. He couldn't be mistaken. One of the men who had treated Joe Grinley to the barbed wire had rope burn on his neck! Was Wes that man? He must be. Few men escaped the noose; there couldn't be two of them around Pincher Creek. And Wes rode for Matt Westwood!

Clint's brain reeled with all the implications. Was Matt behind the attack on Joe? If so, why? And where did Jim Dixon's killing fit in? Were these two men acting for someone else in attacking Joe? But who?

As they rode silently on Cap's trail, Clint puzzled over the whole affair. What did he know about Wes and Buck? Very little. Westwood had taken them on about a month ago. Said he was merely increasing his number of riders. Yet Clint could not recall any men looking for work at that time. Had these two been brought in for a special purpose? Strange that they should be on hand when news of Jim Dixon's killing had been brought into town and so joined the posse. Clint figured he would have to do some quick checking once he was back in town.

But now he must see that the capture of Sam Grinley was carried out successfully without anyone getting hurt for he was beginning to reinforce his doubts about Sam being behind the rifle which had killed Dixon. But Sam had run and the finger of suspicion pointed at him.

Seeing Cap move into the deeper shadows, the three riders quickened their pace to keep him in sight. Their progress was steady, matching their pace to his, pausing when he paused, engaging the utmost precaution so as not to betray their presence, and using whatever cover they could to get nearer to Cap.

Their quarry stopped and they turned behind an outcrop of rock. As had been their practice throughout their trailing, Clint and Wes slipped out of the saddles, leaving Buck in charge of the horses, while they took up a position from which they could watch Cap.

They were puzzled by his continued

examination of the rock-face and kept his actions under careful scrutiny. They stiffened into complete immobility when they saw him turn away from the left-hand side of the valley, but relaxed again as he worked his way to the opposite side.

'What the hell's he looking for?'

'Some sign of Sam's whereabouts?' suggested Clint.

The two men scrutinized Clint's every move.

'What now?' queried Wes, when Cap dismounted. Almost before they realized it Cap had disappeared into the rock face. 'Come on, we'll lose him!' came Wes's urgent whisper as he started to scramble to his feet.

Clint grasped his arm and pulled him back down. 'Not yet,' insisted the marshal. 'He's left his horse. He'll be back.'

Wes curbed his eagerness not to lose sight of Cap. The lawman was right, Cap would be back. The moments ticked by. Wes was becoming anxious. A job had to be done and he wanted no slip-ups.

Suddenly Cap reappeared, bringing the tension of anticipated action back to the two men.

'No Sam,' muttered Wes with annoyance.

He started to turn to Buck and the horses to be ready to take up the trailing again.

'Wait!' Clint's urgent whisper brought Wes's attention sharply back to Cap. 'He's on to something.'

Cap was leading his horse towards the cleft.

'Got it!' gasped Clint as Cap's action took his mind tumbling back to a brief moment when he had laughed at young Sam's enthusiasm about a secret valley. 'The way to Sam's valley and no way out but this! We've got him!'

The information came with the thrust of a rapier to Wes's mind and in the briefest of moments he had the situation sized up. He whirled. 'Rifle!' The word, only a little above a whisper, was piercing, bringing an instant reaction from Buck. He leaned over and in one and the same moment swept the rifle from Wes's scabbard and tossed it to him.

As he caught it Wes channelled a bullet into the breech and swept round drawing Cap into his sights.

Everything had happened so swiftly that Clint was caught unawares, just as the rifle came to Wes's shoulder he started to react. But his movement to stop Wes was frozen by a sharp command, 'Don't!' Clint found himself staring into the cold muzzle of Buck's Colt trained unswervingly at him.

His eyes widened in amazement. 'What the...?'

The words were lost in the crash of the rifle. With the sound springing back and forth between the walls of rock, echoing skywards to be lost in the stone talons of the bird of prey, Clint stared unbelievingly at the sight of Cap spinning to the ground. Scared by sudden noise the horse went into a run dragging Cap with it.

'What the hell?' Clint's rugged face darkened with a rough anger. But before either Wes or Buck made a reply the realization of an almost certain possibility thundered at Clint's mind. 'That was one hell of a rifle shot!' he gasped. 'And Dixon's killing must have been!' His eyes widened at Wes. 'You!'

Wes's face broke into a broad grin. 'Right, fella, but knowing ain't going to be of much use to you!' As the last word died on his lips he swung the rifle held at waist height, and squeezed the trigger.

The shot tore a great hole in the marshal's stomach and blasted him backwards. He crashed to the ground not knowing that his blood stained the rocks and earth.

'Wal,' grinned Wes. 'We've got Sam Grinley to ourselves, Buck. After the pay-off we'll head north.'

'Sure thing,' laughed Buck. 'This one's been dead easy. Come on let's go.' Wes came to his horse, slid his rifle back into its leather and swung up into the saddle. The two men set their mounts towards the cleft.

Sam stirred from his drowsiness. The tensions of yesterday, the exertion of the ride in his weakened state, the heat on his back had all contested the desire for sleep throughout the night. Daylight had brought only a fitful alleviation of that desire. Sam started into full awakening. Something had stirred him. He had heard it again.

He inclined his head, trying to pick up the sound again above the murmuring of the stream. There! A scraping. From the direction of the cleft! A startled panic seized Sam. He scrambled to his feet and hurried to his horse. Casting anxious glances towards the cleft, he led the animal behind a spur of rock.

Someone coming? But who? Who had found his secret valley? He licked his lips anxiously and glanced towards the rifle butt protruding from his saddle. He had escaped the horror of killing a man by the merest fraction of a second, but what now? Were pursuers approaching? Would he have to kill to survive? And if he survived what life would there be? Beads of sweat trickled down his temples. His hands were clammy. He wiped the palms down the front of his shirt and turned to his rifle. His fingers closed round the butt slowly. He hesitated, then a decision made, he gripped the rifle firmly and drew it from its leather.

He glanced towards the cleft. No one had emerged from the gap in the rock. He must find himself a better position. He shrugged off the soreness in his back and crossed the hundred yards to a mound which sloped towards the rock face to his right. He climbed it quickly to a boulder-strewn ledge which gave him a commanding view of the ground towards the cleft. Settling himself comfortably behind one of the boulders, he laid his rifle beside him and waited.

The moments dragged on seeming to reach to endless time. With each of them the gnawing hollow in the pit of Sam's stomach worsened. He felt a sudden rising within him and it took all his determination to stave it off. Whatever happened he must not succumb to unmanly feelings. He was here because of his pa, he did not regret it but he'd do it again. He'd not give way now. His pa would still be proud of him.

With his thoughts reaching out he almost missed the first movements. He stiffened. His heart-beat raced faster. He swallowed hard, and narrowed his eyes to speed his gaze across the distance, bringing the two men, who led their horses from the cleft, into sharp focus.

Who the hell? He had expected to see the marshal, Clint Holmes, but instead two strang– No. He had seen them some place. Pincher Creek. New men. Riders for Matt Westwood. About a month ago. He'd heard their names. Buck, Wes. What the hell were they doing here? Sit tight. They might go.

Sam licked his dried lips and kept the two men under close scrutiny. They stood surveying the small valley. Sam saw them exchange words and wished he had been near enough to overhear them. The thinner man motioned to the left and his companion, after securing the horses near the entrance to the cleft, removed the rifles from the leather and handed one to the other man, Wes, as Sam put a name to him.

The cold hand of fear closed round his heart. The men were staying. There was purpose in their rifles, a caution in their movements. They were stalkers! He was the quarry! The realization that he was involved in a game of life or death jolted his nerves. He gripped his rifle harder, drawing a reassurance from its feel. He wanted to be treated as a man – well, he'd got just that. He had to act like one. What would his pa have done in this situation?

Sam found a cool reasoning returning to his mind. He looked around him. He was in a fairly strong position. Neither man could get round and behind him without being at the mercy of his rifle. But two, with forces split might be able to pull something to get the advantage. He must stay alert for any possible manoeuvre which would put them in a position to kill him.

But why Wes and Buck? Why Matt Westwood's men? Why were they seeking him? Why not the law?

'Sam! Sam Grinley!'

Sam started at the sound of his name. Quiet. Don't answer. Don't betray your whereabouts, not yet, not until it was necessary.

'Sam! We know you're here,' shouted Wes. 'Better if you come quietly.'

Sam did not reply. He watched the men,

alert, ready to mark a position should an answer come.

Sam did not reply.

'Sam! Sam Grinley. There's a big posse out after you, better for you to come quietly with us rather than have us bring them to hunt you down.'

Silence greeted the suggestion. Wes waited a few moments then crouched down on his haunches, cradling his rifle in his arms. Buck sat on a rock about twenty yards to Wes's left.

The minutes moved steadily on. Sam mopped the sweat from his face. Were they going to make it a war of nerves? Sit it out expecting their threatening presence to break him? Well, he'd show them. He'd play them at their own game. He'd not give way. He settled himself into a more comfortable position, expecting a long wait.

Ten minutes seemed years.

Wes straightened slowly. He drew himself to his full height, with feet astride, perfectly balanced. The rifle was held ready for instant action. The picture of the determined hunter who gets his prey was conveyed in his attitude, while Buck's stocky, tough appearance as he stood in a slight crouch, gave the impression of a tenacity to get what he was after.

Sam's lips tightened. How could he hope to survive? Men, experienced. They'd hunted and killed before. Sam stared at them. Nothing more certain. The menace of death was in their very attitude. Would it be wiser to give himself up? After all he hadn't killed Jim Dixon. But would they believe him? Would the law? Where the hell was the law? Why these two?

Sam's puzzled mind suddenly seemed drawn to the rifle held by Wes. It seemed to loom large. It seemed to dominate the whole of his vision. A rifle shot. Jim Dixon falling. His own rifle unfired. Could the rifle large in Wes's hands be the one which had killed Dixon? But if so why had these two come after him? Had they seen him at the Lazy Y? Or was it a case of, knowing of his threats directed at Jim Dixon, they wanted him to take the blame. But how had they known? Matt Westwood. They rode for Matt Westwood. Hell, was he behind all this? Had he had his pa and Jim Dixon killed? Had he put them on his trail? But how? No doubt he'd be investigated after Dixon's death, and be found missing. But how had they traced him here?

Sam's thoughts suddenly exploded. If they

had killed Dixon and now wanted him they would have no intention of taking him alive. Dead he would be blamed for Dixon's death. He'd run. He'd pointed the finger of suspicion at himself and they had seized that chance. Well, let them try. He'd show them! He tightened the grip on his rifle. He alerted his whole being and put the two back into focus.

'Sam Grinley, this is your last chance.' Wes's voice came sharp and clear. 'Give yourself up and no harm will come to you. If not we're coming to get you.'

Only the running water answered.

'Grinley, you're only a kid. We don't want to gun down a kid.'

Sam's jaw tightened. Kid! Damn you! I'll show you who's a kid! The rifle came to Sam's shoulder. He squinted down the sights. Wes. He squeezed the trigger. The sound crashed around the valley. The bullet spanged the rock close to Wes. Both men dived for cover.

Damn you! Damn you! Sam cursed. He'd fallen for the taunt. He'd betrayed his whereabouts in anger.

'All right, Buck, take him dead or alive.' Wes emphasized the word dead, conveying Sam's fate to him.

Two shots came in quick succession from Buck, whining over Sam's head. Two more came. Sam cowered, but he caught a glimpse of Wes breaking from his cover. Sam let off a rapid shot which sent Wes seeking protection again.

Every nerve in Sam's body tightened as silence settled down again. He must be watchful, ready for any move by the men below.

Cap stirred. Some feeling came back to him. His head throbbed, his body ached. He flicked his eyes open. Everything was in a mist. Where was he? What had happened? What had he been doing?

He closed his eyes hoping it would ease the thunder in his head. It did not. He still had the feeling of a herd of steers pounding through him. His eyes came open slowly. Everything whirled. Faster and faster in on itself. Suddenly it stopped. He stared at a brightness overhead. Black walls pushed it upwards. He moved his head slightly, seeking more identification. A bird! A menacing bird! A swooping eagle! Automatically he moved to protect himself. The sharp ache which came with the movement served to clear his mind further.

Eagle! The rock bird. Eagle Rock!

Everything which had happened flooded back into Cap's mind.

Sam. He had been trailing him. The cleft! He was leading his horse to it. The crash of a shot and almost in the same instance he was falling with his mind plunging into impenetrable darkness.

Cap sat up shakily. He raised his hand to his temple and felt sticky blood which oozed from the deep gash. He thanked his luck. A fraction closer and he would have been dead. Instead he had been knocked unconscious. He glanced at the wall of rock, seeking the cleft. It was about fifty yards away, and judging by the pains in his body the horse had dragged him over the rough ground before the reins had left his hand.

He moved his legs, his arms, turned his head and felt his ribs. Nothing broken. Bruising and lacerations where his clothes had been torn but nothing worse. Slipping the bandanna from his neck he wiped the blood from his face.

With his thoughts clear came the demanding question, who had fired the shot? Sam? Cap was doubtful. It had come after he had emerged from the cleft to get his horse. That meant someone knew he was there, and that signified that he had been followed.

He cursed himself for a careless fool. Someone must have kept watch on the Circle T in case he knew something of Sam's whereabouts. The marshal had been smart, playing all the possibilities. Cap frowned as he scrambled to his feet. But if the law was involved, why shoot him? His head swam, misting his thoughts. He tensed himself, fighting the dizziness. Slowly his mind cleared. He looked round for his horse and saw it about a hundred yards away towards the head of the valley.

His movement, as he started for the horse, startled two buzzards and sent them flying for the higher rocks, with a loud beating of wings. Cap froze, staring after the birds. He glanced back towards the spot from which they had risen. The ground was hidden by a boulder. Cap turned and walked slowly towards the place.

'My God! Clint Holmes!' The sight of the gory body, its stomach blasted open, shook Cap. The lawman dead! 'Then who the hell shot at me?' he muttered, 'and then killed Clint!' Cap's thoughts raced. There had been no shot before the one which almost killed him so the marshal had been killed later. By whom? Someone who didn't want

Sam taken alive. Someone who wanted to put the blame for Dixon's killing on him. And now Sam would get the blame for killing the marshal while resisting arrest. The killer had seen him come out of the cleft and, in his eagerness to return, the killer had read the signs that he had discovered Sam.

In the desperate need to get to Sam in the shortest possible time Cap, ignored his aches and pains ran to his horse. He grabbed his rifle and raced for the cleft. Better to leave his mount than have to spend time cajoling it through the cleft.

He reached the cutting and hurried between the towering walls of rock. He had gone only a few yards when a rifle shot resounded from somewhere ahead. Shot after shot came, merging into one cacophony of echoing sound, mocking Cap with the possibility of its meaning. He pressed forward faster, hoping he would not be too late. The cleft seemed to stretch interminably as each twist and turn revealed only another one ahead. Then suddenly the end was there. The cleft widened slightly and ended abruptly.

Cap stopped. His chest heaved, drawing air deep into his lungs. Though everything urged him to dash because time was precious and even a few seconds delay could be disastrous, Cap forced himself to be calm. He had to exercise caution. Impetuous action would be just as disastrous.

He moved slowly forward, his rifle held low against his waist ready for action. More and more of the small valley came slowly into view. He froze. Two horses stood to the left. Two riders. Cap's mouth set in a grim line. Sam was up against the odds. Cap hoped he was not too late to change that to evens.

He remained where he was. A movement might betray his presence and he did not want the advantage he held to pass to someone else. He kept as much of the valley as he could see under constant surveillance, hoping he would be able to determine the position of the two men.

A rifle sent the noise of a shot crashing around the rocks. It came from a knoll and brought a hope to Cap for it had been aimed somewhere to Cap's right. Sam must be alive and Cap now knew the approximate position of one of Sam's pursuers. If only he knew where the other one was. As if in answer to his wish a rifle, away to Cap's left, roared twice. Almost in the same instant he caught a movement about fifty yards to his right. It was only a glimpse but it betrayed the position of a man who had moved from one cover to another closing in towards the knoll while his companion kept Sam preoccupied. And in that glimpse he had identified Wes Dilland.

So the rifleman was Buck Masters. Cap quickly surveyed the ground. Then, as two more shots were fired, knowing the two men would be preoccupied, he covered the only piece of open ground in a running crouch. He flattened himself against a huge boulder, breathing deeply as the anxious moments passed. The rifle crashed again and Cap breathed more freely. He had not been seen.

He edged round the boulder and weaved a way stealthily between the rocks. The rifle boomed repeatedly. Cap saw Wes burst from his cover and make a dash to a group of rocks at the foot of the knoll. Cap's nerves tensed. Now Wes had complete cover all the way to the top of the knoll! The fall of the terrain prevented Sam from seeing his stalker. Unless Cap acted quickly and accurately Sam would be doomed.

Keeping low, Cap moved quickly round two more rocks and climbed a short slope between two huge boulders. As he neared the top of the slope, he saw it gave on to a flat ledge, the side of which was lined with rocks, giving Buck adequate cover from which he could keep firing at the top of the knoll without danger to himself.

Cap did not hesitate. His actions were precise and swift. Two strides took him across the ledge. He jabbed his rifle into Buck's back. 'Freeze!' he hissed. Startled, Buck started to turn until a further jab reminded him of what Cap wanted. He stiffened.

'Leave it!' rapped Cap and Buck's hands came slowly from his rifle. 'Turn round.' As Buck turned, Cap brought the stock of his rifle sharply upwards, taking him on the chin. Buck did not even have time to identify the man who had got the drop on him before his mind went blank.

Cap turned his attention quickly to Wes. He was three quarters of the way to the top. Cap's only hope of saving Sam was a rifle shot but he could not get an accurate line from where he was. In order to do so he would have to forsake the cover of the rocks and that would throw him into a clear view for Sam's rifle.

Wes was climbing quickly. He knew he was hidden from Sam's sight and therefore could move without the cover of his sidekick's rifle.

Cap knew he could not waste a moment, that his shot would have to be quickly made and it would have to be accurate. He charged every nerve in his body to this objective.

In one flowing movement, he stepped out of the cover, brought his rifle to his shoulder and sighted on the climbing man.

A rifle crashed. A bullet whined close to Cap's head, but he ignored it as he remained fixed on his target and squeezed the trigger. Almost in the same instant he saw Wes jerk, lose his balance and tumble back against the rocks.

The rifle on the knoll spat again but Cap was already diving for cover and the shot whined harmlessly overhead.

Cap rolled over and, easing himself on to his elbows, raised his head to shout, 'Sam, hold it! Cap here!'

'Cap!' yelled Sam.

'Yeah. It's me!' called Cap. 'Take it easy. I might have only winged that fella climbing to get you. Stay put!'

'Right!' shouted Sam.

Cap turned his attention to Buck. He removed the Colt from the holster and picked up the rifle. He glanced across at the knoll and could see no sign of movement from Wes. Cap left the ledge and, alert for any reaction from Sam's would-be assassin, ran quickly towards the foot of the knoll. Reaching it without incident, Cap scrambled upwards, aiming towards the spot where he had last seen the man fall. He dropped Buck's Colt and rifle and held his own rifle ready for action.

Cautiously alert Cap stepped round the rocks making his way upwards. Suddenly he froze in his step. Wes sprawled a few feet away, Cap scrutinized him quickly, then relaxed. Wes was dead.

'Sam! Sam!' yelled Cap. 'Get on down here!'

'Right,' came the eager reply.

Sam came scrambling down, sending stones and earth showering in front of him.

'Cap. Am I mighty glad to see you!' he grinned. He stopped when the body came into view. 'How about Buck Masters?' he asked anxiously.

'Unconscious back yonder,' replied Cap. 'I needed one of them alive to testify. Let's get to him.'

'Then it was you I fired at,' gasped Sam.

'Yep, and mighty close you were,' replied Cap. 'I had to risk it otherwise I wouldn't have got Wes.'

'I'm sorry,' Sam apologized quickly with a look of horrified concern of what he might have done.

'You did the only thing,' Cap was quick to reassure him.

'How did you find me?' asked Sam.

'Your ma said you sometimes came to the hills with your pa, and Abbe remembered you telling her about the secret valley and about Eagle Rock. So I came, hoping I could soon pick up the right lead.'

They reached the unconscious Buck. 'I can't figure out how he and Wes found me.'

'Followed me,' replied Cap.

Sam stared at Cap in astonishment.

Cap told him quickly about the posse. 'I figured the marshal and these two must have stayed to watch the house in case we knew something about you. They followed me. One of them took a shot at me after I had found the way into this place and went back for my horse.'

'Then where's the marshal?' queried Sam.

'Dead. They must have shot him after they shot me.'

'But why?' puzzled Sam. 'Why kill the marshal?'

''Cos he'd have taken you alive. They wanted you dead.'

Sam frowned.

'I figure it this way,' explained Cap, 'With you dead you could still be blamed for Jim Dixon's death and also the marshal's – shot when you were trying to escape. I reckon these two are responsible for Jim Dixon's killing.'

'But they ride for Matt Westwood.'

'Sure. I reckon Buck'll provide a few answers. Get their horses.'

Sam hurried away to fetch the animals while Cap carried Buck away from the ledge and clear of the rocks.

When they had Buck tied up they slung him across the saddle of one of the horses and led the two animals to the foot of the knoll. Cap brought the body down, placed it over the saddle of the second horse and tied it on.

When he was satisfied, he removed the bandanna from Wes's neck.

'Sam, come here,' he called.

Sam left the other horse and when he reached Cap the older man pointed to Wes Dilland's neck.

'Rope burn,' said Cap. 'Your pa told me that one of the men whom he caught erecting that wire, who rolled him in it, had a rope burn on his neck!'

ELEVEN

The sound of a horse brought Kate Grinley hurrying on to the veranda. She wanted more than one rider. She wanted Cap and Sam. But maybe this was Sam.

She shielded her eyes against the late afternoon sun. This wasn't Sam. She brushed away a wisp of hair from her eyes and screwed them against the brightness, bringing the rider's silhouette into sharper focus.

The man, big, broad, sat heavily in the saddle. Only one man in these parts filled a saddle that way – Matt Westwood.

Kate sighed and waited. Remembering the meeting after the funeral, Kate could guess what had prompted this visit.

'Howd'y ma'm,' Matt touched the brim of his Stetson as he stopped his horse in front of the veranda.

Kate nodded in reply then asked, 'What brings you here, Mr Westwood?'

'I think we can dispense with the formalities. We've known each other long enough, Kate.'

'Very well, Matt,' replied Kate, with an almost imperceptible nod, though her voice showed no change in her emotion.

Matt swung his huge frame out of the saddle, flicked the reins round the hitching rail and stamped up the steps. He pulled his kerchief out of his pocket and removed his Stetson to wipe the sweat from his forehead.

'It is mighty hot, Kate,' Matt commented as he flopped into a chair.

Kate crossed to the door of the house, pushed it open slightly and called out, 'Abbe, fetch Mister Westwood a drink of water.' She turned and let the door swing shut. 'Sorry, I've nothing stronger, Matt. I saw what it did to Joe.'

Matt dismissed the matter with a move of his hand. Abbe appeared with a jug and a glass of water and placed it on the table beside Matt.

'Thanks, Abbe,' said Matt.

'Run along Abbe, Mr Westwood and I have things to talk over,' said Kate.

As the door closed behind Abbe, Matt glanced at Kate. 'You're a mighty perceptive woman, Kate.'

'Doesn't take much figuring, Matt,' replied Kate. 'You ain't a regular visitor here.'

'Well, thought any more about selling?'

'No. But the answer's still no.'

'But, Kate surely the situation's changed.'

'Has it?'

Matt was taken aback by Kate's attitude.

'With Sam killing Jim Dixon.'

'Did he?'

'He's on the run isn't he?'

Kate fought to keep her feelings to herself but her fingers, fiddling agitatedly with her wedding ring, gave her away.

'You ain't seen him since the shooting?' said Matt. 'Then why run if he didn't do it?'

'Oh, I don't know,' cried Kate, tears dampening her eyes. 'I just don't know.'

'Well, one thing's certain, you can't run this ranch without a man. So I suggest you sell out to me while my offer's still a good one, can't tell what'll be in a few days time.'

Kate straightened her back, drawing on a steel-like determination not to give way to her feelings in front of Matt Westwood.

'I don't believe Sam shot Jim Dixon,' she said firmly. 'So why he's run I don't know. But I'll tell you this, Matt, when he returns we'll run this ranch.'

'Don't fool yourself, Kate. Sam threatened Jim after Joe's death. Several people heard him.'

'Maybe, but that doesn't mean he killed Dixon.'

'That doesn't, but it throws a strong lean towards Sam.'

Kate made no reply. Matt, seeing the grim set of her mouth, pushed himself out of the chair. His broad, powerful frame towered over her.

'Remember my offer, Kate. You'd be wise to act on it quickly.'

Again Kate did not answer. Matt turned to the steps as he crammed his Stetson back on his head.

A few moments later, as he rode away Kate gave way to her feelings and cried.

The tears eventually gave way to fitful sobs and then silence.

Kate woke with a start. Someone was shaking her. 'Ma! Ma!' The urgency in Abbe's voice penetrated the mists bemusing her mind.

Suddenly Kate was wide awake. She sat upright in her chair. Abbe was sitting at her feet shaking her by the knee.

'How long have I slept?' she asked, her eyes widening.

'You've had a good sleep, Ma.'

'Must have,' Kate shivered. The sun was lowering. She stretched.

'Ma, there's someone coming.'

Kate froze. 'Where?'

'Over there,' Abbe pointed.

Kate relaxed and pushed herself out of the chair. She stared across the grassland in the direction indicated by Abbe. 'I can't see anyone,' she said.

'I just caught a glimpse before they dropped into the hollow,' replied Abbe, coming beside her mother at the rail.

'How many?' asked Kate.

'Not sure,' answered Abbe.

'More than one?'

'Yes.'

'More than two?' pressed Kate anxiously.

'Think so.'

Kate's heart missed a beat. More than two. The posse? Why return here unless... Kate stopped her worst thoughts. This was no good. She must not start thinking that way. Whoever the riders were they would soon be here and then she would know. She stared towards the rim of the hollow anxiously awaiting the forms to break the skyline.

Although she was expecting them they seemed to appear suddenly, catching her unawares. One. Two. She counted them silently. Three. The fourth and fifth were pack horses. They came nearer slowly. Kate watched with fixed eyes. Pack-horses. They weren't pack-horses. Saddle-horses with something slung over their backs. A cold hand clutched at Kate's heart. Sam! Oh, no! One of them couldn't be Sam!

As if in answer to her doubts one of the riders broke away from the rest by putting his horse into a gallop. Kate's heart leaped. She'd know that sit of a galloping horse anywhere. She had watched it so many times as Joe and Sam raced the last mile home.

'Sam!' The word escaped from Kate's lips in a cry of ecstasy. 'It's Sam. Come on, Abbe.' With that she was down the steps and running. With all the joy that she knew, she raced across the dry earth towards the galloping rider who loomed larger and larger.

Then he was there, hauling his mount to a dust-stirring halt. Sam thudded to the ground before the animal stopped and flung himself into his mother's arms.

'Ma! Ma!' he cried.

She hugged him tight as tears of joy flowed down her cheeks, and Abbe hugged them both.

'Sam, are you all right?' Kate asked as she eased him gently from her so she could see for herself. There was all the concern of an anxious mother in her voice.

'Sure,' grinned Sam.

'You didn't...' Kate faltered, hesitating to put her query into words. But Sam read the unspoken question.

'No, Ma, I didn't kill Dixon.'

Kate hugged him again in her relief at the truth. 'Cap find you?'

'Yes. And thanks, Abbe, for telling him.' He grinned at his sister.

'Who else?' asked Kate glancing in the direction of the riders.

'It's a long story, Ma.'

A few moments later Cap was stopping the horses in front of them.

'Hello, Kate,' smiled Cap.

'Thanks, Cap.' The deep sincerity in Kate's two words made no other appreciation necessary. She glanced at the other rider, who had remained sullenly silent, and was startled to see Buck Masters with his hands tied. Her eyes flashed to the other horses but she could not see who was slung across the saddles. She looked back at Cap with a query in her eyes.

'The marshal,' said Cap.

'Oh, no!' gasped Kate shocked that the lawman had been killed. 'How? Why?'

'The other's Wes Dilland,' said Cap,

ignoring Kate's question.

'I said it was a long story, Ma,' said Sam quietly.

'And Matt Westwood's riders. He was here earlier today.'

'What for, Ma?' questioned Sam, some alarm showing in his tone.

'Pressing me to sell.'

'You didn't.' Sam's alarm heightened.

'No. Told him you'd be running it.'

'How did he take that?' asked Cap leaning on his saddle-horn.

'Didn't like it. Implied Sam wouldn't be coming back.'

'Did he!' mused Cap as he exchanged glances with Sam. 'Where did he go when he left here?'

'Can't be certain but he took the trail to town.'

'Reckon I'll head right on it,' said Cap to Sam. 'You can stay and tell your ma everything.'

'I'm riding with you, Cap,' said Sam.

'Could be trouble,' warned Cap.

'Used to that now,' grinned Sam. 'Seeing me just might upset Westwood. With Masters to testify we might force him into the open.'

'Could be something in what you say,'

agreed Cap, but, seeing Kate's restraining hand on Sam's arm he hesitated to approve.

'Ma, I've got to see this through,' said Sam turning to look deep into his mother's eyes. She stared back without speaking for she saw that Sam was no longer a youngster. He was a man who could make his own decisions in these situations. Her hand slid slowly from his arm in silent resignation to the inevitable passage of time.

Sam kissed her on the cheek. 'Won't be long, Ma.' He winked at Abbe, turned and swung into the saddle.

Mother and daughter watched them until they disappeared from sight then walked slowly back to the house.

Some oil lamps were competing with the last remnants of daylight as Cap and Sam, leading the other three horses, rode into Pincher Creek.

In only a matter of moments the word that the marshal was dead and Sam Grinley was riding in spread rapidly through the town. A crowd had gathered outside the marshal's office by the time the horses reached the building. Queries and speculations were rife amidst the curiosity of the folk who pressed around on all sides.

'What the hell happened?' queried Bert Shelldon who, at the sight of the marshal's body, reckoned he was now the man with full responsibility for law and order in Pincher Creek.

'Buck Masters and Wes Dilland killed the marshal,' replied Cap. 'Sorry about Wes, it was necessary.'

Shelldon swung his gaze on Sam. 'And you, Grinley? Giving yourself up?' The deputy sensed there was much more behind the arrival of these riders and held back from making an immediate arrest. He had left Masters and Dilland with the marshal keeping an eye on the Circle T hoping Cap Millet would lead them to Sam. Now the marshal and Dilland were dead, Masters a prisoner, accused of murder and Sam free.

'No,' replied Sam tersely. 'I ain't done anything.'

'What the hell's going on?' The bulky shape of Matt Westwood pushed his way through the crowd to the side of the deputy. 'Get Grinley arrested for killing Dixon,' he snapped, 'and Millet for killing Wes.'

'Ain't any use, Westwood,' rapped Cap. 'The game's up, Buck talked.'

'I did…' The words were snapped back in Buck's throat as Cap swung his hand hard

216

across Buck's mouth.

'No one asked you,' snapped Cap, hoping the start of Buck's denial hadn't alerted Westwood.

But the rancher had picked up the hint and alert to seize on any chance by which he could extract himself from the situation suddenly yelled, 'Look out, Sam's gun!' Westwood's gun was clearing its leather, the hand bringing it round on Buck aiming at silencing him on the pretext of stopping Sam.

Cap flung himself sideways crashing into Buck. The report of Westwood's Colt sent the crowd scattering. Cap felt a sharp pain in his upper arm as he and Buck crashed to the ground between the horses.

Even as Westwood got his shot off, Bert Shelldon's gun was clearing leather. 'Hold it!' he rapped harshly. 'There'll be no more killing.'

Westwood finding himself staring into the muzzle of a lawman's gun straightened.

'What the hell are you trying, Westwood. Sam ain't wearing a gun.'

'He was after Buck,' said Cap pushing himself to his feet and indicating a wound on his arm.

'There's a lot of explaining to do, so let's

have you all inside.' Bert's voice came with a command which would stand no nonsense.

Once inside the marshal's office Cap explained what had happened in the hills.

When he had finished Shelldon looked at Buck Masters. 'This true?'

Buck hesitated sullenly but, in those few moments, realized he must try to ferret a way out of this for himself. 'Go easy on me if I talk?'

'Depends,' rapped the deputy.

Buck licked his lips apprehensively. He caught the condemning look in Westwood's narrowed eyes. Talk and some day you'll get it. But Buck figured he could be long gone before Westwood could carry out the unspoken threat.

'Westwood had Wes and myself to do some rough riding if necessary. When he saw his ambitions of a big powerful ranch, able to fence a large area, able to run with enough riders to resist any encroachment by nesters, being thwarted by Dixon and Grinley, he sent us into action. We got rid of Grinley but didn't expect his widow and son to aim at running the Circle T. But Sam's threat to Dixon provided us with the opportunity to get rid of Dixon and blaming Sam. We could kill Sam saying he had resisted arrest. Then both ranches would be open for Westwood to take over. It was working that way. What happened in the hills is as Cap told you and the bits he guessed at are just about right.'

Shelldon glanced at Westwood. 'Anything to say?'

Westwood shrugged his massive shoulders. 'What's the use?'

'Then you and Masters better keep each other company in the cells.'

Kate heard the thunder of the hoofbeats and hurried outside. The dark forms of two riders came at the ranch-house at a gallop. They hauled their horses to a halt and swung from the saddles.

'I used to beat pa home too,' panted Sam amidst his laughter.

Kate smiled as she welcomed the two men. 'The table's set. You've a lot to tell me while we eat.'

The publishers hope that this book has given you enjoyable reading. Large Print Books are especially designed to be as easy to see and hold as possible. If you wish a complete list of our books please ask at your local library or write directly to:

Dales Large Print Books
Magna House, Long Preston,
Skipton, North Yorkshire.
BD23 4ND

This Large Print Book, for people
who cannot read normal print,
is published under the auspices of

THE ULVERSCROFT FOUNDATION

3196
3292